RIDING A CHAMPION

Kate let Southwood canter a few strides, then put him back into a trot. She turned him toward a giant log.

"She can't jump that from a *trot*," Stevie said anxiously. "It looks four feet tall."

But Kate knew she could. Southwood trotted up and over the log as though it were a cross rail. Kate halted him and began to quietly walk him up the hill to the stable, her face beaming with joy.

"It's been so long!" she called to Beatrice. "And it felt so good! Thank you."

Beatrice smiled again, a sharp smile. "Why don't you ride Southwood this weekend?" she asked, her voice ringing out across the yard.

Kate gasped. That bank jump she had just taken had been perfect, absolutely perfect, and Southwood was a wonderful horse. She would only ride in this one show. It didn't have to be the way it was before.

"Oh, Kate," Carole said, her face aglow with happiness for her friend. "You should do it."

"We'll help you," Lisa promised.

"All right," Kate said. "I will."

Also available by Bonnie Bryant:

Watch out for a completely new series, PONY TAILS. If you love THE SADDLE CLUB, then you'll definitely love PONY TAILS, published by Bantam Books – for horse-lovers everywhere!

THE SADDLE CLUB

GOLD MEDAL
RIDER

BONNIE BRYANT

A BANTAM BOOK
NEW YORK · TORONTO · LONDON · SYDNEY · AUCKLAND

THE SADDLE CLUB: GOLD MEDAL RIDER
A BANTAM BOOK : 0 553 50443 6

First published in USA by Bantam Skylark Books
First publication in Great Britain

PRINTING HISTORY
Bantam edition published 1996

With thanks to the management and staff at Snowball Farm
Equestrian Centre for their help in the preparation of the cover

Bantam Books are published by Transworld Publishers Ltd,

61–63 Uxbridge Road, Ealing, London W5 5SA,
in Australia by Transworld Publishers (Australia) Pty Ltd,
15–25 Helles Avenue, Moorebank, NSW 2170,
and in New Zealand by Transworld Publishers (NZ) Ltd,
3 William Pickering Drive, Albany, Auckland.

Printed and bound in Great Britain by
Cox & Wyman Ltd, Reading, Berkshire.

*I would like to express my special thanks
to Kimberly Brubaker Bradley
for her help in the writing of this book.*

1

"THANKS, MOM!" STEVIE LAKE shut the car door and ran through the warm spring rain to the front door of her best friend Lisa Atwood's house. Carole Hanson, Stevie's other best friend, followed close on her heels.

"Whew!" The girls reached the shelter of the Atwoods' front porch. Carole shook raindrops from her black hair. "Do you think Lisa's expecting us?" She rang the doorbell.

"We haven't missed a day yet, have we? I hope she's feeling better." Lisa had come down with chicken pox exactly one week earlier. She woke up on a Saturday morning, covered with spots and scratching. Stevie and Carole had both already had chicken pox, so they could visit Lisa without worrying about catching it.

1

"Come on in, girls," Mrs. Atwood told them when she opened the door. "Lisa's in her room. I was just about to make her some lunch. Have you eaten?"

"We're fine, Mrs. Atwood," Carole said politely. "We came straight from Pine Hollow, and we brought our sandwiches with us. We decided not to stay after the Horse Wise meeting." Pine Hollow was the stable where all three girls took riding lessons and where Stevie and Carole boarded their horses. Horse Wise, the Pony Club where they learned about horses and riding, met there on Saturday mornings. Usually Stevie, Carole, and Lisa ate lunch at the stable and rode all afternoon.

Stevie nodded in agreement. Reaching under her rain poncho, she opened the backpack she'd been keeping dry, and pulled out a brown paper bag. It was smushed into the shape of a Frisbee, and something purple dripped from one corner. Stevie grimaced and quickly put the sack back. She must have sat on it during Horse Wise.

"That's okay," Carole said, "I'll share." She confidently patted the pocket of her raincoat, but as she did so her face fell. Her pocket was empty. She tried to remember where she'd left her lunch. She had been in her horse's stall when Stevie called out that her mother was there to give them a ride to Lisa's. Carole remembered opening her lunch bag, giving Starlight an apple, and setting the rest of the lunch down to give the gelding a big hug. Her lunch was still in

2

Starlight's stall. "I hope Starlight likes tuna salad," she said ruefully.

Mrs. Atwood smiled. "Never mind, girls, I'll fix you something, too. Go cheer up Lisa."

Stevie and Carole thanked her and hurried upstairs. "Isn't that just like us!" Stevie exclaimed. "We need Lisa around to keep us straightened out."

The three friends complemented each other well. They all loved horses and riding, but otherwise they were quite different. Lisa was logical and coolheaded. She hadn't been riding as long as the others, but she worked very hard at it and was doing well. Stevie was serious about only one thing—horses. She treated the rest of life as if it were one big practical joke. Even though Lisa and Carole sometimes had to fish her out of her own hot water, they agreed that life was more exciting with Stevie around.

Carole was the best rider among them. She knew she'd make horses her life—someday, somehow. She tried hard to learn absolutely everything about them; and because she was so focused on them, she often forgot other things. Leaving her lunch behind was typical.

When the three friends were together, they made a great team, and they knew it. They had formed The Saddle Club, dedicated to horses, riding, and each other. Members had to be horse-crazy and always ready to help one another.

Carole knocked softly on Lisa's bedroom door. "It's us," she said.

"Come in." Lisa was slumped in the pink armchair between her bed and a window. She was wearing a raggedy old pair of sweats and looked cross and disgruntled. Her face and hands were covered with red scabs.

"I felt glad this morning because it was raining and I knew you wouldn't be able to ride, so you would come see me," Lisa said as her friends took off their rain gear. "Then I felt horrible for wanting the rain to spoil your fun. Then I felt glad again, because I'm tired of being home and I wanted someone to talk to. And then I felt horrible, because what I really want to do is go riding with you guys. I'm sorry it rained!"

Carole and Stevie both gave her a hug. "Which are you now?" Stevie asked. "Glad or horrible?"

"Both." Lisa crossed her arms over her chest. She looked wretched.

"The pox will go away soon," Stevie pointed out. "The doctor said you might be able to ride next week."

"*Maybe* I'll get to ride," Lisa said. "But the pox won't go away soon. I'm going to look crusty for a month."

Stevie raised an eyebrow. "That could be an asset," she said seriously. "Simon Atherton asked about you after Pony Club. He seemed really concerned."

Lisa and Carole giggled. Simon was a dorky boy who

4

rode at Pine Hollow. Lisa would be glad for anything that would keep Simon from following her around.

"Don't let Stevie scare you, Lisa," Carole said. "I don't think Simon's really interested in you. He's still mooning over Veronica."

"Sometimes Simon reminds me of Drew," Stevie said thoughtfully. "Nice, but dorky." Drew was a groom who worked for friends of theirs, Dorothy DeSoto and Nigel Hawthorne.

"Drew's not dorky!" Lisa protested. "He's practically a grown-up, anyway. How can you call him that when he loves horses so much?"

"He's a dork-head," Stevie persisted.

"Speaking of dork-heads," Carole cut in, "Stevie's got something that should really cheer you up." She sat down on the edge of Lisa's bed.

"That's right!" Stevie dug into her backpack and pulled out a large envelope, which she tossed onto Lisa's lap. "It only took me five months to remember to get them developed. Pictures!"

"Of our trip to North Carolina?" Lisa ripped open the envelope. Stevie and Carole exchanged grins. It was the first time they'd seen Lisa act enthusiastic all week.

"Oh, look! Here's one of Dorothy and Nigel!" Lisa held up a snapshot of an attractive couple sitting on a hay bale.

Carole took the photo from Lisa and studied it closely.

5

Dorothy was Carole's hero. She had started riding at Pine Hollow, just like The Saddle Club. She had grown up to be a famous rider, and had been at the top of her professional career when a freak accident left her unable to show. Now she was married to a British event rider, Nigel Hawthorne. The couple trained horses and riders at their farm on Long Island in the summer and in Southern Pines, North Carolina, in the winter. The Saddle Club had visited them in Southern Pines several months earlier.

"Here's grumpy Beatrice," said Stevie, pointing to a picture of one of Dorothy and Nigel's students. "She's not smiling in any of them."

"Typical," Lisa remarked. "I'm really sorry about what happened to her, but it wouldn't have hurt her to smile once in a while."

"Here's Drew with that dopey look on his face. Looks like he's admiring you," Carole said, pulling a photo off the pile and handing it to Lisa.

"He's not admiring me," Lisa protested, looking at the picture. "He's admiring Southwood. And you shouldn't call him dopey—"

"Dorky," murmured Stevie.

"He's nice and I like him," Lisa said firmly. "He's a friend."

Stevie grinned wryly. "I know. He is nice. He's just such an easy target!"

"Look," Carole cut in. "It's Kate and Southwood!" Kate

6

Devine was the fourth member of The Saddle Club. She lived out West on a ranch with her parents, but she had gone with the other girls to North Carolina. Southwood was a championship horse, and Kate had been lucky enough to ride him in a competition there.

The three bent over the photograph. "Wow!" Lisa said. "It's amazing!" She turned her bedside lamp on and held the photo under it. "Kate's position is perfect, and you can tell what a huge effort Southwood made over the fence."

"Look at Kate's expression," Carole added. "Look how determined she looks."

"I sure hope Southwood makes it to the Olympics some day," Stevie said. "We'll be able to say we knew him before he was famous."

Lisa brushed her hair from her face and smiled. "Boy," she said, "that was a great trip." The girls sat back with contented sighs. They could remember everything as clearly as if it had just happened. . . .

2

The Previous November . . .

A COLD WIND blew the last autumn leaves off the trees that lined the road. "It's not fair!" Stevie's twin brother, Alex, repeated. Stevie ignored him. Her mother's car bounced along the gravel road toward Willow Creek's small airport and pulled up next to the tiny terminal. Lisa and Carole and their parents were standing outside.

"At last!" Stevie got out of the car and waved to the others. She had thought she would be late for sure. Her mother had had a meeting after work, Stevie couldn't find her second-best breeches, and at the last minute Alex had insisted on coming with them. Stevie was convinced that he only wanted to come so that he could whine all the way there. Sometimes she really liked having Alex for a twin. This was not one of those times.

Stevie pulled her duffel bag out of the trunk. Alex grabbed her backpack. "Careful with that," Stevie told him. "It's got my camera in it."

"I can't believe you get to miss school," Alex grumbled. "It's not fair!"

"Your sister did very well on her report card this quarter," Mrs. Lake said, closing the trunk and putting her arm around Stevie's shoulders, "and she hasn't been sick once this year. Missing one day of school isn't going to hurt her."

Stevie grinned at Alex. She had no idea why her report card was so good—her teachers did seem to have a sense of humor this year, which helped—but she was pretty relieved about it. Usually her report card skirted right on the edge of disaster—disaster being any grade below a C, because if she got one of those she wasn't allowed to ride. This term—wonder of wonders—Stevie had gotten nothing below a B. Two teachers had even seen fit to give her As!

It was a Thursday evening in late November, and the next day there was a countywide teacher's convention, so all the schools would be closed. By missing school on Monday, The Saddle Club would get to spend four days with Dorothy and Nigel in Southern Pines.

Stevie hurried to join her friends, who stood near the end of the runway. Colonel Hanson, Carole's father, checked his watch. "Any minute now," he murmured.

"Lisa, dear," said Lisa's mother, "did you remember to pack a nice dress for evenings?"

Lisa didn't answer. Stevie could tell from the look on Lisa's face that she had not packed a nice dress. Neither had Stevie. No way would they need dresses, nice or otherwise, around Dorothy and Nigel.

"I hope you brought your blue one," Mrs. Atwood said. "It's so nice for fall. It might be chilly in the evenings, you know, even in North Carolina."

"I know, Mom." Lisa sighed. She was trying hard to ignore her mother's questions without seeming rude. Clothes were important to Mrs. Atwood, and horses were something she did not understand. Sometimes Lisa and her mother seemed exactly opposite.

She thought for a moment. Her blue dress was with her other dresses, hanging in her closet at home, but where were her muck boots? Suddenly she was afraid she'd forgotten them, and she would need them when she helped Dorothy and Nigel clean stalls.

Lisa dropped to her knees and unzipped her duffel bag. She searched through it quickly—riding boots, hard hat, crop. All her gear took up so much space. Aha! Here were her muck boots—only they were still mucky. Lisa looked at the dried dirt crumbing onto her sweaters and smiled to herself. Where she was going, no one would notice a little dirt—or even a lot of it. She zipped her duffel.

"All set, dear?" asked her mother.

"All set, Mom," Lisa assured her. It was true, too, even though Lisa and her mother had different definitions of "all set."

Carole squeezed Lisa's arm. "I just remembered something," she whispered. "I forgot my toothbrush!"

Lisa laughed. "Again?" Carole always left something behind. One summer she'd gone by herself to visit Dorothy and Nigel on Long Island. She'd forgotten her toothbrush then, too. It was like old times.

"I'm sure you can buy a toothbrush in Southern Pines," Stevie said, moving to Carole's side. "Look! Isn't that the plane?" The three friends stood shoulder to shoulder, watching a small light in the evening dusk grow bigger as it approached them.

"That's it!" Colonel Hanson said. "You girls be nice to Kate's father now, and stay out of his way on that plane. Don't drive the businessmen crazy."

"I wonder if any of them ride?" Carole asked mischievously. "If not, we could tell them what they're missing."

"I wonder if any of them know any good jokes?" Stevie added, grinning at Colonel Hanson. "If not, I could tell

11

them the one about the green-eyed hermit and the three-toed frog."

Carole's father laughed. He and Stevie shared the same weird sense of humor.

"I'm sure the girls will behave," Mrs. Atwood said sweetly, with a warning look at Lisa.

"I think we'll be pretty busy catching up with Kate," Lisa replied sensibly. "We probably won't even notice the businessmen."

A small yellow plane touched down on the far end of the runway and came screeching to a halt not far from where they stood. After a moment the door opened, stairs descended, and a tall girl, slightly older than the rest of The Saddle Club, tumbled out.

"Carole, Stevie!" she cried. "Lisa!"

"Kate!" they screeched and ran to greet her. The four girls hugged on the runway, whooping with joy.

"It's been so long since we saw you," Carole said, giving Kate another hug. Kate's father had been in the Marines with Colonel Hanson before he retired and bought a dude ranch out West. The Saddle Club had been there several times. Colonel Devine was also a private pilot for a man who often flew to the Washington, D.C., area, so he was sometimes able to fly The Saddle Club to his ranch or bring Kate to them in Virginia.

"Hey, Mitch! Good to see you, buddy." Colonel Devine came out of the plane and shook hands with Carole's father. He shook hands with Stevie's and Lisa's parents, too. "Been riding any horses lately?" he asked Mrs. Atwood affectionately.

"I'm saving myself for a return trip to the Bar None," Lisa's mother replied with dignity. They all laughed. The last time The Saddle Club had visited Kate, all their parents had come with them to the ranch.

"I can't believe your dad could arrange to fly us this weekend," Stevie said as the girls stowed their baggage in the plane's hold. They turned and said good-bye to their parents and to Alex, who was still complaining, and followed Kate and her father into the plane. Three men in golf sweaters sat inside.

"It was easy," Kate said. She led them to the back four seats, and they all fastened their seat belts. "We're ready, Dad!" She introduced her friends to the three men and explained where they were going. "These gentlemen are friends of Dad's, and they hired him to take them golfing for the weekend. There's some place right near Southern Pines that's good for golf, and Dad's going to stay with them and play, too. He said he could stop here and drop me off to visit you, but I knew your friends Dorothy and Nigel might be in North Carolina, so I checked it out, and they were! Dorothy was really nice on the phone, even though she doesn't know me. She said they'd love to see us all. So it was easy, even if it was at the last minute."

Lisa was puzzled. "How did you know Dorothy and Nigel

might be in North Carolina? Usually they're on Long Island."

Kate laughed. "Half the eventers on the East Coast spend the winter in the South, and most of those go to Southern Pines," she said. "They don't want to try to keep their horses fit in the snow. You can't gallop in indoor arenas—there isn't room."

Lisa wrinkled her nose. "But how would you know that?" she asked.

"Don't forget Kate's history," Carole reminded her.

"That's right," Kate said, laughing. "Long ago, I even spent a few winters in Southern Pines, North Carolina. That was before I learned not to take myself so seriously."

"Oh, right." Lisa felt embarrassed. She always had such a great time hanging out with Kate that she forgot Kate had been one of the best junior event riders in the country. Carole had told them all how famous Kate had been, but Lisa had never seen her that way, and Kate rarely talked about her riding past.

"Don't feel silly," Kate said. "That's been behind me for a long time. I prefer just riding for fun. But you guys will love North Carolina. It's a gorgeous state to ride in."

While Kate described the pine forests and sandy hills of southern North Carolina, the little plane chugged forward into the fading light. It was dark when they arrived and saw Dorothy and Nigel waiting on the tarmac.

14

"Dorothy! Nigel!" Carole called to them from the door-way of the plane. Dorothy and Nigel waved back. Nigel was wearing a Norwegian sweater and a baseball cap along with breeches and riding boots. He was even wearing spurs. Dorothy wore jeans and a jacket. She still rode occasion-ally, despite her injured back, but she did most of her horse training from the ground.

"This is our friend Kate Devine," Carole said.

"We feel like we know you already," Dorothy said pleas-antly, a smile lighting her face.

"I say," said Nigel, shaking Kate's hand, "you look famil-iar. Don't I know you from somewhere?"

"You should," Dorothy chided him. "Kate's one of the best junior eventers around." She smiled at Kate. "Nigel wasn't in the United States back when you were compet-ing, but I remember seeing you at several competitions. And, of course, Carole, Stevie, and Lisa have told us all about you."

"I *used* to be an event rider," Kate said to Nigel, a small but firm smile on her face. "I don't compete anymore. I just ride for fun."

"Well, we're glad to meet you," Nigel said. "Any friend of The Saddle Club is a friend of ours."

The girls chattered enthusiastically while they gathered up their belongings. Kate said a quick good-bye to her fa-ther, and they all piled into Dorothy's car. It was a tight fit. Lisa sat on Kate's lap, and Carole sat on Stevie's.

15

"It isn't a long drive," Nigel assured them. He hit a pothole and Lisa's head bumped the roof. "Bouncy, though." They all laughed.

"Maybe you should have brought horses to the airport," Stevie suggested. "We could have ridden back instead."

"I'd have had to bring my best jumpers," Nigel said, shaking his head as he hit another bump. "These roads are horrendous."

As they drove, Dorothy told them a little bit about Southern Pines. "It's a great place to train horses. Not only is the weather pleasant, but there's lots of open land to train on. There's a big national forest with open bridle trails, and you can reach it from our stable."

"So many eventers come to this part of the country in the winter," Nigel added, "that the last events of the fall and the first events of the spring are held right around here."

The Saddle Club knew that "events" were a type of horse show that tested all of a horse's capabilities. In a three-day event, the horse performed a dressage test on the first day, which showed off its elegance, beautiful movement, and perfect obedience. On the next day the horse galloped over a cross-country course of solid fences to prove its jumping ability, stamina, and speed. On the final day the horse competed over a course of show jumps, which would fall if the horse so much as brushed them.

This tested the horse's jumping style, precision, and accuracy. Eventing was a complete test of the horse's skills.

"Are there any events here this weekend?" Lisa asked.

"As a matter of fact, yes," said Nigel. "One of the last horse trials of the year starts on Saturday, and we're entered. You'll get to see Campfire, one of my young horses, go."

"What about Southwood?" Carole asked, remembering the beautiful young horse she'd ridden when she had visited Dorothy's farm. "Will we see Southwood?"

Dorothy and Nigel exchanged uneasy glances. Nigel frowned.

"Maybe," Dorothy said at last.

"I hope not," Nigel added. "But probably you will."

NIGEL TURNED DOWN a long gravel driveway. "Here we are!" he said. The pine trees thinned, and the girls could see a small white house and a very large barn. "Do you want to unpack first?" he asked them. "I can show you where you're going to sleep. Or are you guys hungry? We could order a pizza."

The Saddle Club exchanged glances. "Let's go see the horses first," Stevie said. The others nodded.

Dorothy roared with laughter. Nigel shook his head, grinning. "Five bucks," Dorothy said to him. "Hand it over." Nigel took out his wallet.

"I should have known better," he said. To the girls he

explained, "Dorothy made a bet with me that you'd head straight for the stable no matter how late you got here."

"And you thought we wouldn't?" Kate sounded amazed. "I mean, I know you don't know me very well yet, but you know them." She nodded her head toward her friends.

"I know, I know," Nigel replied. "Don't rub it in. Follow Doro to the horses. I'll do bellboy duty and toss your bags on the porch. I'll be right with you."

Dorothy led them through a small door in the side of the giant barn. "It's not quite as big as it looks," Dorothy said. "But we've got an indoor arena. See, the lights are on." The Saddle Club could see a yellow glow spilling into the main aisle halfway down. "We share the stable with another couple, David and Karen. All of their horses are on the far side, past the entrance to the arena, and all of our horses are down here." Dorothy snapped on the aisle lights.

"Wow!" Carole turned on her heel, looking around her. "What a lot of horses!" One by one, the horses stuck their heads over the tops of their half doors: chestnuts, bays, blacks, and grays—all beautiful horses, all in top condition.

"You've got almost as many horses here as there are at Pine Hollow!" Stevie said.

Dorothy smiled. "Not quite. But we do have quite a few. Happily, our business is growing."

"Do they all belong to you?" Lisa asked. She couldn't keep the wistful tone out of her voice. She knew she wasn't really ready to have her own horse, but she wanted one so much!

Nigel, coming into the stable, heard her question. "No, no," he said, laughing. "Maybe half. And most of those are very young horses that we're just beginning to train. Some of the others belong to students of ours, who'll come down here to ride after Thanksgiving and Christmas, and the rest are owned by people who don't ride but like to own show horses."

"Like Lord Yawelkesleigh," Lisa said, remembering the evil man whose horses Nigel had ridden in England. His name looked ridiculous, but it was pronounced simply "Yaxley."

"Yes, like Yawelkesleigh, but not entirely," Nigel said, a faint grin flitting across his face. "To the best of my knowledge, none of my current owners is a criminal." Lord Yawelkesleigh had been sent to jail after plotting to kill his horse for insurance money.

"Aren't any of your students here with you now?" asked Stevie. She could understand people wanting to be home for the holidays, but it was still a few weeks until Thanksgiving.

"Sure," Nigel said, sending another grin in Dorothy's direction. "One is. My very *fav*-or-ite student of all."

"She's in the indoor arena now," Dorothy said. "Still practicing." Lisa thought she could hear a note of disapproval in Dorothy's voice.

"Beatrice," Carole guessed, from the way Nigel made the word "favorite" sound about eighteen syllables long. Beatrice was Southwood's stuffy, horrid, and, she had to admit, talented owner. When she wasn't around, Nigel usually pronounced "Be-a-tri-ce" the same stretched-out way. He made it sound longer than "Mississippi."

"The one and only," Nigel said dryly. They continued down the aisle toward the entrance to the arena. "Most higher-level event riders give their horses a vacation at this time of year because there aren't any competitions between early December and February. But not dear Beatrice. She doesn't believe in vacations—at least not for her horse."

Nigel dropped his voice as they reached the gate of the arena. Under the strong lights a horse and rider were trotting in perfect harmony. Nigel raised his voice again, and sounded cheerful. "Hullo, Beatrice," he said. "How's things?"

"Is she—," Stevie began. Carole elbowed her into silence as Beatrice and Southwood swept past the gate.

"Shhh! Yes, she's the girl I told you about."

"And that's *Southwood*? The horse you rode in a show?" Lisa's voice squeaked. "He's gorgeous!"

Carole looked at the horse in confusion. "Yes—I guess so—I mean, it must be him, his markings are the same. But he didn't look like *that* when I rode him." Carole remembered Southwood as a beautiful horse that jumped with enthusiasm, but that was gentle, almost sleepy. The sleek

21

dark bay horse Beatrice was riding now looked fiery and powerful. It *was* the same horse, Carole realized. Southwood had changed.

Beatrice turned Southwood down the center line so that he was trotting directly toward the girls. Slowly she shortened his stride until his trot was nearly vertical. Both Beatrice and Southwood were concentrating intently. When they reached the exact center of the arena, Southwood lengthened his stride and began to move diagonally.

"Half-pass," Kate whispered. "He does it beautifully."

Stevie nodded. She'd seen the dressage move performed before. "Incredible," she whispered back. Southwood had world-class presence, and he and Beatrice moved in complete, total harmony. Stevie hoped that someday she could ride her own horse, Belle, that well.

"You rode this horse?" Lisa repeated, looking at Carole with astonishment.

Carole started to laugh. In the arena, Beatrice brought Southwood to a walk and loosened the reins. Southwood stretched his neck and snorted. Carole turned to her friends. "When I rode him he wasn't like this, believe me," she said. "He was sweet."

"He's still sweet," Nigel said. "It's just that he's come a long way since you rode him, Carole. He hadn't even evented then. Now Beatrice rides him at advanced level."

"How many of your horses are that good, Nigel?" Lisa asked.

22

"Right now, he's the only advanced-level horse I have," Nigel said. "They're very rare. Horses have to be incredibly athletic and have tremendous mental toughness and determination to make it to that level."

"I remember," Kate said, her eyes shining in a way the rest of The Saddle Club had never seen before. "Great event horses love jumping fences more than anything else in the world. They think they can do anything. The really great ones *can* do just about anything."

"Heart," Nigel said, summing it up. "The best horses are all heart."

"I remember," Kate repeated softly. She rarely spoke about her past as a competitive rider. She'd stopped competing when she realized that she'd lost sight of what was important—having fun. For a while, whenever Kate was in the saddle, all she could think about was winning—and not even winning, really, as much as beating everyone else. The problem was, beating everyone else wasn't much fun. After a while nothing about riding had been fun. The Saddle Club had helped her learn to enjoy horses again. Kate was very grateful to her friends. She gave a small sigh. She was much happier now.

Carole and Stevie heard the sigh and exchanged glances. They'd never heard Kate talk so much about competitions as she had in the past hour. Stevie thought Kate's sigh sounded like regret. That made perfect sense to Stevie—she loved to win, and she found Kate's decision

23

not to compete hard to understand. Maybe this weekend would rekindle Kate's competitive fire. After all, why should Kate let her talents go to waste?

"Pound Sterling," Carole said out of nowhere, interrupting Stevie's thoughts. "Lord Yawelkesleigh's horse. He was an advanced horse, wasn't he, Nigel? Are you still riding him?" Carole would never forget the silver stallion she'd seen Nigel ride in an event in England.

Nigel sighed. "No and no," he answered. "Lord Yawelkesleigh's in jail, as you know. I don't ride for him at all now, and I heard that Lady Yawelkesleigh sold all the Yawelkesleigh horses to the New Zealand event team. Pound Sterling had a lot of heart and talent, and I think he'll make it to the advanced level, but he wasn't there yet. You saw him in a preliminary-level event."

"Preliminary! That means beginner," Lisa objected. "Those jumps were huge! They can't have been for beginners."

Dorothy rejoined them after filling a horse's water bucket. "In eventing, 'preliminary' doesn't mean beginner," she explained. "There are six levels of eventing. Preliminary is in the middle, and advanced is the highest."

"You can't skip levels," Kate added. "You've got to start your horse at the bottom and earn the right to move up. You aren't allowed to rush your horse."

Beatrice had gotten off Southwood and was walking to the gate. She overheard Kate. "We don't have to worry

24

about that around here," she said in a loud, rude voice. "The one thing I've learned for sure is that Nigel Hawthorne would never, ever, rush a horse." She unlatched the gate and pulled Southwood through. "It's too bad you aren't more worried about winning," she said directly to Nigel. "Then maybe there'd be a few more advanced horses in this barn."

Lisa thought she could hear a thud as all The Saddle Club's chins dropped to the floor. Never, ever, could they imagine talking to a riding instructor like that, especially one as good as Nigel. Dorothy looked unhappy.

Nigel, however, didn't appear even to notice Beatrice's remark. He stood back to give Southwood plenty of room and patted the steaming horse on the hip as he passed. Lisa couldn't believe it. How could Nigel stand someone so obnoxious? Carole bit her lip. She remembered Beatrice's unpleasant personality from before. Apparently Beatrice hadn't improved with age.

Beatrice tugged on Southwood's reins and began to move him past them. Then she stopped. Turning back to Nigel, she said in the same haughty, challenging voice, "You *will* ride him this weekend, won't you?"

Now Nigel did look unhappy. Slowly, unwillingly, he nodded. "Good," Beatrice snapped, with a humorless smile. Halfway down the aisle, she dropped Southwood's reins to the ground. "Drew!" Beatrice shouted. "Where are you?"

The girls saw a tall, gawky young man come out of the

tack room. He stumbled over a bale of hay. "Golly, Beatrice, I was just cleaning your cross-country saddle," he said. "I didn't realize you were done."

"Well, pay attention next time," Beatrice snapped. She stood with her hands on her hips as the young man loosened Southwood's girth and ran the stirrups up on their leathers. "And cool him out completely. If he colics it'll be your fault!" Beatrice's boots clicked sharply as she walked out the door. A moment later an engine revved, and through the glass window on the door they could see a sleek sports car, with Beatrice driving, tearing away from the stable, spraying gravel as it went. The young man murmured to Southwood and softly stroked his nose.

"Ugh," Stevie said. "She can really ride, but *ugh!*"

"I told you so," Carole said. "That's exactly what she was like when I met her at Dorothy and Nigel's farm on Long Island."

Now Nigel looked downcast. Dorothy put her arm around him. "Don't be upset," she said to her husband. "I understand how you feel, but Southwood is ready. He'll be fine."

Nigel opened his mouth to speak, then closed it and shook his head. "I hope so," he said at last.

"What's wrong with Southwood?" Carole asked.

"Nothing." Nigel began to walk down the stable aisle. The rest of them followed him silently. When they reached Southwood, Dorothy quickly felt the horse's chest to see how hot he was. Drew lifted the saddle from South-wood's back. Without saying a word, the four girls began to help: Carole and Kate took off Southwood's leg boots, Stevie replaced his bridle with a halter, and Lisa threw a cooler over his sweating back. Drew seemed flustered. "Thank you," he said. "You don't have to—I can get that—really—but thank you." He fluttered his hands at them. "I can get it. Really."

"We like to help," Lisa told him. He was so awkward that she felt sorry for him.

"Drew, your sudden helpers are our guests for the weekend," Dorothy explained. "Girls, this is Drew Gustafs, our fantastic groom and Southwood's best friend. Drew, this is The Saddle Club—Kate, Carole, Stevie, and Lisa."

Drew looked skinnier close up than he had from farther away. He had a mop of wiry mouse-brown hair that stood out from his head. One of his eyebrows was higher than the other, and he had a tiny scar on the corner of his mouth. His eyes were kind, and even though he seemed shy he had a nice smile. "Thanks," he said again, with a duck of his head. "I better get Southwood cooled out." He clucked to the horse and led him out of the barn.

"He seems more comfortable with the horse than with people," Kate remarked as they watched him go.

Dorothy chuckled. "I think he is."

"What's wrong with Southwood?" Carole repeated.

27

Nigel massaged his forehead. "He's fine," he said. "The problem is that Beatrice expects too much from him. He's a tremendously talented horse, but he's very young and he's just now qualified for the advanced level. Beatrice wants him to do as much as possible as quickly as possible. Above all, she wants him to win. I think she should slow down. Southwood has plenty of time. If she makes him compete in difficult events before he's entirely ready, she could end up scaring him or even hurting him. If they have an accident it'll take a long time for him to regain his confidence. By going too fast, Beatrice could slow him down in the long run."

"Beatrice and Nigel both think Southwood can go all the way," Dorothy explained. "They just have different ideas about how to get him there."

The girls looked at one another. "I'll ask," Lisa said finally. "What do you mean by 'all the way'?"

"What do you think, Kate?" Nigel asked. "I bet you know what we mean."

"The Olympic Games," Kate said. She shrugged and smiled. "What else?"

"Wow," Stevie said. "Really? Southwood in the Olympics? That'll be so cool!"

Carole looked stunned. "I rode an Olympic horse?" she asked.

Nigel held up his hands. "Hold on," he said, laughing. "Not yet, you didn't. It's a very long road to the Olympics,

28

and there are a lot of horses trying to get there. We'll see how Southwood does."

"If you want him to make the Olympic team, you'd better start pushing him," Kate said. "It's a long way from one advanced horse trials to an Olympic event course." The rest of The Saddle Club was a bit surprised at the edge in Kate's voice.

"No," Nigel explained. "We're not trying for next summer's games. Beatrice is aiming for the Olympics four and a half years from now. She really does have plenty of time. She's not going to gain anything by risking Southwood's confidence, not this early.

"There's no point in moving Southwood to advanced level now," Nigel continued. He rubbed his hands together and his voice rose. "This weekend isn't a three-day event—there's no steeplechase, and it's held over two days, so it's called a horse trials. It isn't that big of a deal. There won't be another competition until February, and all the important ones are even later than that. I think Beatrice should skip this event and let Southwood relax a little."

Nigel sighed. He watched Dorothy check a horse and carefully latch the stall door when she was done. "Obviously, Beatrice disagrees with me," he said. "But she can't ride in the trials because she's leaving for the Virgin Islands tomorrow afternoon. Her brother is getting married in Saint Croix on Sunday. That's why she told me to ride him."

"So why did you say yes?" Stevie asked. "I mean, you think it's wrong. Beatrice can't make you ride. She won't even be here."

Dorothy turned off the stable lights, and they stepped outside into the cool night air. Moonlight shone through the pine trees. As they all walked toward the little house, Dorothy reached for Nigel's hand.

"It's a hard thing, Stevie," Nigel said. "But you see, Southwood is a very fine horse. And if I don't ride him, Beatrice will find another trainer who will. She might find another trainer permanently."

The girls understood. Max Regnery, the owner of Pine Hollow, had to take nonsense from some of the people who rode with him, too. The name Veronica diAngelo sprang instantly to mind. She was also a spoiled brat who refused to take care of her own horse. Max needed her business, so he put up with her. Undoubtedly Nigel had to do the same.

"Southwood looked so good," Carole said soothingly. "I'm sure he's more than ready. Don't you think so, Kate?"

Kate shrugged. "Hard to say," she replied. "Events aren't won in the dressage ring. Lots of horses are good at dressage, but the cross-country phase counts the most. It all depends on how well Southwood jumps."

Nigel laughed and gave Kate a soft clout on the head. "He jumps better than he does dressage," he told her.

Kate smiled. "Then he'll do fine."

4

THAT NIGHT CAROLE was unable to sleep. All around her on the floor of Dorothy and Nigel's living room, her friends lay in their sleeping bags, fast asleep; but Carole stared out the window at nothing, too keyed up to close her eyes. This trip was so exciting! She loved spending time around professional riders. And the idea that Southwood might someday go to the Olympics gave her a thrill, even though it wouldn't happen for another four and a half years.

Carole sighed and rolled onto her side. Her eyelids fluttered, just for a second. When she opened them the room was lighter. The sky outside the window looked navy blue. Carole reached for her watch—six A.M.! She must have fallen asleep after all.

31

A light was on in the kitchen. Carole wiggled out of her sleeping bag, wrapped it around her shoulders, and went to investigate. There was a pot of hot coffee on the stove and the light above the sink was on, but the room was empty and the house was quiet. A big box of doughnuts and a carton of orange juice sat on the table. There was a note next to them: "Girls—See you at the stable. D."

Carole set the note down and looked out the window. Dorothy wasn't kidding—they were already up! The lights were on in the stable, and Beatrice's sports car was parked next to Nigel's big truck.

Carole hurried back to the living room, stumbling over the ends of her sleeping bag. "Stevie!" she hissed, shaking her friend by the shoulder.

"Mhmph?" Stevie mumbled, burying her head in her pillow.

Lisa sat up. "What is it?" she asked.

"Time to get up. We're late!"

Kate sat up and without a word began to pull on her breeches. Lisa did the same. Stevie rolled over. "How can we be late this early?" she wailed, but she, too, began to get dressed.

In a few minutes they were hurrying across the yard to the stable. Stevie tucked her camera into her jacket pocket.

"Beatrice is here already?" Stevie whispered, looking at

Beatrice's car. As she spoke, Drew came out of the stable, leading Southwood, who was groomed and saddled. Beatrice followed, pulling on a pair of riding gloves. She settled her helmet over her hair, accepted Southwood's reins from Drew, and vaulted into the saddle. With a cool nod to The Saddle Club, she headed Southwood down the road.

"Good morning, Drew," Kate said.

"G-G-Good morning," Drew stammered. Stevie pulled her camera out and snapped his picture, with the barn in the background. "What'd you do that for?" Drew asked. He blushed and seemed as nervous as he had the night before.

"Sorry," Stevie said cheerfully. "I want lots of photos to remember this trip. Remind me to take some of Southwood when Beatrice comes back."

"He's better-looking than I am," Drew said.

"But I'd much rather have pictures of you than of Beatrice," Stevie replied. Drew blushed again.

"We thought Beatrice was going to the Virgin Islands today," Carole said. "Why is she riding now?"

"She's not leaving until later," he explained. "She's just taking Southwood out for a hack. She doesn't want to do too much with him today, since he's competing tomorrow."

"That's what I mean," Carole said. "Why ride him at all? He's going to get a big workout tomorrow."

"Oh, Carole," Kate cut in before Drew could answer. "Event horses have to be in really good shape. When they're in competition form, they have to be ridden almost every single day."

"I've never seen a horse in such good shape as Southwood," Carole objected. She wasn't trying to argue with her, but surely Kate could see how strong and fit Southwood looked. Carole probably rode Starlight five days out of every week, and Starlight didn't look nearly as well-muscled as Southwood.

"He's in good shape, but he has to stay that way," Kate said. "He's an athlete, just like Nigel."

"I guess that makes sense," Carole agreed.

Dorothy came out of the stable. "Good morning!" she said cheerfully. "Did you sleep well?"

"Too well," Lisa said. "We're sorry we're late."

Dorothy checked her watch and laughed. "It's six-fifteen," she said. "Normal people are not awake at this hour. You aren't late—you're just later than us."

"What can we help you do?" Lisa asked as they followed Dorothy and Drew into the barn. "I wore my muck boots. We could start by cleaning stalls."

Nigel was in the center aisle, grooming a big liver chestnut horse. He grinned at the girls. "Good morning," he called. "I certainly hope you're ready to work."

"As a matter of fact," Dorothy said, "we really do need

34

your help. We'll all be leaving for the show this afternoon, and we have a lot of things to do before then. Would you do us a special favor?"

"Sure," Stevie said instantly, while the others nodded.

Dorothy grinned at her husband. "I really hope we're not asking too much," she said.

"Give it a try," Nigel said. "You know these girls—they'll do anything to be around horses."

Stevie groaned. "Don't tell me. You need the manure pile moved."

Nigel shook his head. "Worse than that, I'm afraid."

Carole grimaced. "I don't know what could be—I mean, whatever it is, we'll do it for you."

"Well . . ." Dorothy hesitated, then finally said, "Would you mind exercising some horses for us this morning?"

Everyone burst out laughing. "Nigel, you really had us going for a moment there," Kate said. "I was thinking the same thing Carole was—what could be worse than moving a manure pile?"

"When I find out, I'll let you know," Nigel promised.

Dorothy took down a clipboard hanging on the wall and consulted it. The girls could see that it was some sort of organizational chart for the horses in the barn. "Lisa, I'm going to give you Panama Red," she said. "He's in the third stall on the left. He's an older guy, but he's a good one, and

I think you'll like him. His owner runs a boutique in New Jersey. She rides with us in the summer and comes down here once or twice in the spring."

Lisa went to meet Panama Red. "He looks like a Thoroughbred," she said, patting the neck of the handsome chestnut horse.

"He should, since he is one," Dorothy replied. "Most of our horses are. Other breeds make good event horses, too, but Thoroughbreds are the best. They have terrific stamina—they can run all day long.

"Let's see." Dorothy consulted her list again. "Stevie, I've got the perfect horse for you. His name is Steve. Second stall on the left, next to Panama."

Stevie laughed. "Hello, Steve," she said. Steve looked at her and blinked.

"His registered name is Stevedore," Dorothy said. "Nigel shortened it."

Carole got a horse named Warrior. Nigel brought saddles and bridles out to them. He explained that Steve and Warrior were both for sale. "They're good, solid horses," he said. "Very well trained, and they've both done preliminary three-day events. But they don't have the jumping ability to move any higher. They'll be great horses for a rider who just wants to have fun."

Kate stood waiting for her horse. "Nigel?" Dorothy called her husband over and pointed to a name on the clipboard. Nigel pressed his lips together, thinking.

36

"If she wants to," he said. "She's good enough to ride him."

"What do you think, Kate?" Dorothy asked. "Are you in the mood for a challenge?"

Kate's face lit up. "Sure!" she said.

Dorothy smiled. "Come meet Giacomo," she said. "He's one of our very young horses, and we think he has enormous potential. Right now, however, he's nervous and excitable. What you should do is try to get him to relax and enjoy himself." She took Kate down the aisle to meet a tall, slender chestnut horse with an enormous white blaze and wild, rolling eyes. Lisa, watching, knew that the very thought of riding Giacomo would make her nervous.

"Hey, buddy," Kate said cheerfully, patting Giacomo's neck. Lisa envied Kate her confidence.

"Who are you riding, Nigel?" Stevie asked.

Nigel snorted. "Giacomo's twin sister—at least as far as personality goes. Her name is Santori."

When they had all brought their horses outside and were ready to mount, the girls could see that Nigel's horse was not really Giacomo's twin in any way except personality. Santori was a small, stout, square-built black mare without a speck of white on her. She shared Giacomo's habit of shying violently whenever something surprised her. "Birds of a feather," Nigel said gaily when a gust of wind caused both Giacomo and Santori to jump sideways a foot.

As they set out, Carole paused to pat Warrior on the

37

neck. He was a beautiful Thoroughbred, and any other time she would have been overjoyed to ride him. But, watching Kate on Giacomo, Carole felt just the slightest bit jealous. Carole was used to being the best rider, and although she didn't put on airs about it, she had to admit that it was a position she enjoyed. Nigel and Dorothy had given Kate the difficult, sensitive horse and had mounted Carole on a comparative plug. All because Kate was—well—Kate Devine. Nigel and Dorothy had never even seen Kate ride, but they knew her reputation. Carole winced. She had always known Kate was a fantastic rider, and how could she be jealous of such a good friend?

"Coming, Carole?" Kate turned Giacomo and trotted him back to Warrior's side. Giacomo danced and snorted, and Kate settled him with a light hand on the reins. "I envy you!" she added, laughing. "You'll get to enjoy this ride. I won't even notice the scenery unless this horse spooks at it." She smiled with such complete friendliness that Carole smiled back, her jealousy forgotten.

They followed a smooth path through miles of piney woods. Lisa rode carefully, letting Panama warm up first and then asking him to trot out long and stretch his neck low.

"You girls are doing a fantastic job," Nigel praised them. "You're all using this as a training ride, not just a trail ride, and that's exactly right." He maneuvered Santori to the

38

back, where Stevie had been keeping Steve last in line. "How's it going back here? Any trouble?"

Stevie shook her head. "I'm watching Kate," she said, pointing in front of her. "I'm trying to see if I can pick up any pointers."

"What have you learned so far?"

"Well," Stevie replied, "what I like best is how Kate never gets fussed, and she never gets thrown off balance. Giacomo still isn't really settling down, but Kate can cope with him without getting him or herself upset. I'm not sure how she does it."

"She's got an excellent seat on a horse," Nigel said. "She also has what all truly great riders have: completely independent hands, seat, and legs. She can move her hands to correct Giacomo without letting her shoulders move at all. Or she can sit back on him without changing the tension in her reins. See what I mean?" Kate used her legs to move Giacomo forward past a potentially scary-looking tree stump. The rest of her position didn't change.

Stevie nodded. "Yeah. It's fantastic, but it makes me feel like I'm not a very good rider. I didn't realize Kate was so much better than the rest of us. We usually see her riding Western and just playing around on her ranch. It's not so obvious then how talented she is."

"Kate's had her own horses and all the training she's wanted for years and years," Nigel said gently. "She has also worked very hard. She's talented, yes, but so are you. Someday you'll ride just as well."

"Thanks," Stevie said. She glowed with pride. Nigel thought she could be as good as Kate!

When they arrived back at the stable after an hour's ride, Beatrice was standing in the yard, still mounted on Southwood. She was talking to Drew, who had brought several hay bales out of the stable and was putting them into the horse trailer to take to the show.

The moment Giacomo saw the hay bales he shied violently, leaping to the side and ducking his head. Kate sat up and pulled on the reins, laughing at his mischief, but she couldn't let him get away with it. She went to work teaching him a lesson. The others watched as she tried several times to get Giacomo to walk past the bales. Giacomo refused to do it, twisting and bucking and tossing his head in the air. Kate remained calm, a small, intense smile on her face. Finally she quit trying to convince Giacomo to go around the bales. Instead she trotted him straight at the bales and jumped him over them. Giacomo leaped into the air with a fierce expression, but jumping the bales seemed to convince him where they weren't dangerous. He snorted and Kate praised him. She turned him and jumped the bales again.

After three or four jumps, Giacomo was quiet. Kate trotted him toward the bales one last time, and he jumped them as calmly as a Pine Hollow lesson pony. Kate dropped the reins on his neck and patted him.

The rest of The Saddle Club had been watching in astonishment. They'd never seen a horse move so quickly from fear to acceptance. Kate was wonderful!

"I hope you didn't mind me doing that," Kate said, looking up at Nigel.

Nigel looked amused. "It was fine," he said.

Beatrice had been watching, too. "Did I meet you last night?" she demanded. "Did you come with them?" She used her crop to point at the rest of The Saddle Club.

"Sure," said Kate, straightening in the saddle. "I'm Kate Devine."

Beatrice frowned. "Have I heard of you?" she asked.

Kate shrugged. "I really couldn't say."

"I think I have heard of you," Beatrice declared. "What level do you ride at? Have you done advanced?"

"It's been a long time," Kate said patiently. "I wasn't old enough for advanced level when I was still competing. I rode the open intermediate three-day at Radnor."

Beatrice nodded as if she understood exactly what this meant. Carole wondered if Beatrice had shown at Radnor, wherever that was. "And?" Beatrice asked sharply.

Kate lifted her chin, and a strange expression, mingled triumph and sadness, flooded her face. "I won it," she said.

Beatrice grinned. Her sudden smile was so contrary to

41

her personality that The Saddle Club was surprised by the change. "What about now?" she asked. "Are you old enough for advanced?"

Kate bit her lip, then nodded. "I just had a birthday."

"Good." In a single fluid motion Beatrice dismounted and flipped Southwood's reins over his head. She held them out to Kate. "Would you like to try Southwood?" she asked.

The Saddle Club saw Kate's face turn pale. Any one of them would have leaped at the chance to ride such a glorious horse. Why was Kate hesitating? Perhaps, Lisa thought, Kate was worried about riding a horse that was so valuable.

Kate felt a hundred different feelings. It would be great to ride a trained event horse again. Riding Giacomo had been enough to remind her of all the wonderful parts of horse training: teaching young horses to overcome their fears, helping them move with grace and energy, getting exactly the right responses from them. The morning's ride had also reminded Kate of all the skills in the saddle that she still had but rarely used at the Bar None. Kate knew she could still compete. But she didn't want to.

On the other hand, riding Southwood once could hardly hurt. It would be fun. Kate looked down at Beatrice. "I-I'd love to," she stammered. She slid off Giacomo, handed his reins to Drew, and mounted Southwood.

The first thing Kate did was stand in the saddle, flexing her heels. She shortened the stirrup leathers, then stood again. "Much better," she said. She gathered up the reins and looked at Beatrice inquiringly.

"Out there," Beatrice said, pointing to a field running down behind the stable. "Try anything you like."

Kate took Southwood down the small slope. A stream ran through the middle of the field. On both sides of it Nigel had built several cross-country jumps. First Kate stayed on the near side of the stream. She trotted Southwood for a few minutes, then asked him to canter. His strides were expressive and elastic—this was what an event horse should feel like! Kate asked Southwood to lengthen his stride and he did it instantly, reaching long and low with his front legs. She sat back, and he came back to her.

She splashed him across the creek, then told him to gallop. The far end of the field came up quicker than she thought it would; she turned the horse and pointed him back to the creek. Nigel had built a small drop fence going into the water. Kate balanced Southwood and went for it. Southwood took the jump eagerly. *Splash!* Going into the water, Kate let the reins run through her fingers, then came forward, gathering them in. One stride, two, three—she sat hard and Southwood gathered himself—four strides, then a huge leap onto a bank fence coming out of the creek.

She let him canter a few strides, then put him back into a trot. She turned him toward a giant log.

"She can't jump that from a *trot*," Stevie said anxiously. "It looks four feet tall."

But Kate knew she could. Southwood trotted up and over the log as though it were a cross rail. Kate halted him and began to quietly walk him up the hill to the stable, her face beaming with joy.

"It's been so long!" she called to Beatrice. "And it felt so good! Thank you."

The Saddle Club had noticed how closely Beatrice watched Kate ride. Beatrice smiled again, a sharp smile. "Why don't you ride Southwood this weekend?" she asked, her voice ringing out across the yard. "You seem a lot more excited about him than Nigel does. I bet you'd be a lot more likely to win."

Kate and the rest of The Saddle Club looked at Nigel. As before, he ignored Beatrice's insult. "Go ahead, if you want to," he said to Kate.

Kate gasped. That bank jump she had just taken had been perfect, absolutely perfect, and Southwood was a wonderful horse. She would only ride in this one show. It didn't have to be the way it was before.

"Oh, Kate," Carole said, her face aglow with happiness for her friend. "You should do it."

"We'll help you," Lisa promised.

"All right," Kate said. "I will."

44

AFTER KATE'S RIDE everyone dismounted. "Come on," Beatrice said to Kate, "I've got the event program in my car. I'll give it to you and tell you all about Southwood."

Kate nodded. "Just a minute. I'll take care of Southwood first."

Beatrice scowled. "Give him to Drew! That's what Drew gets paid to do."

Kate grimaced. She was used to doing everything for her horses. Taking a quick look around and not seeing Drew, Kate said, "He must be busy. I'll just be a minute."

Beatrice tapped her foot. "I don't have a minute," she said. "Get one of your little friends to do it. They do know *something* about horses, don't they?"

Lisa blushed crimson with anger and Stevie seemed ready to explode, but Carole stepped forward quickly. "I'll take Southwood," she offered. To Kate she added softly, "It's all right! And it's not your fault—we all know how she is." Carole was holding Warrior's reins in her right hand. She took Southwood's in her left.

"Geez," Stevie said as Kate walked off with Beatrice, "I used to think you were exaggerating about how horrid Beatrice is, Carole. Now I think you were being too nice!"

"It doesn't matter," Carole said. "What matters is that we help Kate. This is a fantastic opportunity for her! I bet she feels like it's a dream come true."

"I know it would be my dream come true," Lisa said, a rapturous look on her face. "Imagine being such a good rider that even people like Beatrice offer to let you ride their horses! You know Beatrice isn't doing it out of the kindness of her heart."

"I'm not sure she has a heart," muttered Stevie. "She doesn't even want to take care of her horse!"

"Exactly," Lisa said. "But Kate cares about horses and she's as good a rider as Beatrice."

"I wish Kate could ride Southwood in the Olympics, instead of Beatrice," Carole said. "Kate deserves it more."

There was a small silence while the three of them looked at each other.

"Are you thinking what I'm thinking?" Lisa asked.

"Only if you're thinking that Kate could ride in the Olympics," Stevie said, a huge grin lighting up her face.

"Not on Southwood, of course," Carole said. "But in four and a half years, Kate could find another horse and train it. I really think she could do it!"

"It's a great idea," Lisa said, "and we can all help her. Shall we make it a Saddle Club project?"

"Of course!" They clapped each other's hands high above their heads in what they called a high fifteen.

"Our first job," Stevie said thoughtfully, "is to get Kate excited about the Olympics. She used to say she'd never compete again, but she did just agree to ride Southwood. We need to get her thinking about how much fun the Olympics would be."

"I agree," Carole said. "But that's not our *first* job. Our first job is to take care of these horses, including Southwood. After all, we do know *something* about horses!"

THE HORSES WERE settled in their stalls eating hay by the time Kate came back. "Beatrice left for Saint Croix," she said to Nigel. "She told me a lot about Southwood, but I hope you'll help me, too. I know how hard this is going to be."

"Of course," Nigel said. "It'll be fun. Believe me, I'd rather teach you than Beatrice!"

"Stevie called her the Queen Bee," Kate said. She

looked thoughtful. "I don't like it when she's rude, but I'm pleased that she's trusting me with her horse. She said that she doesn't necessarily expect me to win, but she thinks Southwood should come pretty close."

Nigel frowned. "I wouldn't worry too much about winning. Not that I doubt your riding skills, or Southwood's ability, but you're both making a big jump going up to advanced level. Besides, winning isn't the most important thing here."

"I know that," Kate said, with a little laugh. "The most important thing is beating the person in second place."

Nigel's face darkened.

"That was a joke, Nigel," Kate added hastily.

"Okay," he said. "It just didn't sound like one. Carole's getting Southwood ready for the trip. Go see how she's doing, will you?"

Nigel still looked bothered by Kate's remark. "But it was a joke," Kate repeated to herself. Or was it? She shook her head once abruptly, as if trying to clear her thoughts. It was a joke. Winning wasn't everything. "No," she said to herself again, "beating the person in second place counts for something, too."

Here it goes, Kate thought. *It's starting already*. Only this time she knew what could happen. This time she could make herself be different. It didn't have to be the way it was before.

She hurried to Southwood's stall. Just outside his door,

drawn in the dust, were five overlapping rings. Inside, Carole was carefully wrapping Southwood's legs in shipping bandages. "Carole, I'm sorry! I didn't mean for you to do all my work!" Kate was still worried about her conversation with Nigel, and her voice came out high and distressed.

"Don't be silly." Carole rose to give Kate a hug. "We're all so happy for you. This is such a great chance for you to get back into competitive riding! And we always like to help one another—you know that. You've helped us with things a hundred times. Plus, we understood how important it was for you to talk to Beatrice before she left."

"She told me a lot," Kate agreed. She sat back on her heels. "But there's still a lot I don't know. Thanks for your help, Carole. Please remember, though—this isn't a chance for me to start competing again. It's just one event. Just one. And what are those rings in the dirt outside Southwood's door? They look like Olympic rings."

Carole bit her lip. "Umm—I think Stevie put those there. For Southwood—you know, because he'll be trying for the Olympics in a few years." She knew that Stevie had really drawn the rings for Kate, but looking at Kate's unhappy face, Carole didn't think her friend wanted to hear that now. She would wait until Kate was enjoying the competition before she really started talking about her being an Olympian.

When they were finished with Southwood, Kate and Carole returned to the tack room. The others were already there, packing tack trunks with gear according to Dorothy's giant list. "Seven bridles," Stevie said, checking them off on the list. "Nigel, we're only bringing two horses—Southwood and Campfire. What are the extra five for?"

Nigel chuckled. "Two horses, three phases," he said. "The horses wear different bridles for dressage and cross-country. For show jumping they wear the same as cross-country, but we do need extras. What if something breaks?"

"What if I end up swimming in the water jump?" Kate added, sitting down with a laugh. "I'll need a dry bridle for show jumping."

"You won't fall off," Lisa assured her. Lisa knew that all riders fell off sometimes, but she didn't think that someone with Kate's skill would ever fall off in competition.

"Oh, I might," Kate answered. She didn't look at all bothered. "Eventers crash a lot. Bigger fences, faster speeds. Speaking of which, Beatrice said I could borrow her saddles and tack, but her riding clothes are too big for me. Do you have any I can borrow, Dorothy?"

Dorothy grimaced. "Not really. I so seldom get on a horse these days that I left all my old stuff on Long Island. Let me see if Karen has some extras." She left the room.

"Karen and David are the other people that share this stable," Nigel explained. "I'm surprised they aren't here to pack yet. That's their half of the tack room over there, and

I know they're going to the horse trials. Karen's riding two horses in your division, Kate."

Stevie continued to pack gear into the trunks. "There's so much stuff," she said. "We never need this much gear for the shows around Pine Hollow—at least not the ones I've ridden in."

"This is different," Nigel agreed. "It's not that this is more important, but it's bigger."

"Major-league riding," Lisa said.

"That's it."

"Olympic riding," Carole added.

"Says who?" came a deep, unfamiliar voice from the aisle. "We're not saying the word 'Olympic' yet, are we? Nigel, shush them. You'll jinx us all!" A laughing man with dark brown hair came into the room.

"This is David," Nigel announced. He introduced the girls. "And here's his wife, Karen."

"And yes, you can borrow some clothes," said Karen. She was a thin woman with long blond hair tied back in a ponytail. "One of you can, anyway. Who's Kate?"

Kate and Karen were about the same size. "This should be easy," Karen said. "Come back to my trailer and we'll get you suited up. Did you bring your own boots?" She put her arm around Kate's shoulder as they walked away.

"How many horses are you taking to the trials?" Lisa asked, noticing the enormous number of tack trunks David was opening.

51

"Four," he said, grunting as he tried to move a trunk from the wall. "Two each, plus Karen's meeting a client there, so she'll actually ride three."

Carole shook her head. "It's so much work just to get my own horse ready when we go to a show," she said. "I don't know how I'd cope with more than one." Carole thought that she would have to learn how if she wanted to be a professional rider.

"It can be hard," David said. "Well, 'hard' isn't exactly the right word. It's confusing at first, but once you get organized it's just a lot of work. You just keep working, all day long."

"For instance," Nigel added, "if you girls hadn't been here today, we still would have needed to exercise all our horses before we left. I would have ponied a few—that means I'd ride one while leading another—and I would have had to get up even earlier than I did to make sure they all got done."

"Beatrice could have ridden one for you," Lisa suggested.

David and Nigel exchanged glances. Nigel grimaced and David laughed. "I don't know how you put up with her," David said. "I know she can pay a lot for good horses and good training, but I still don't see how you stand her."

"She's a strange case," Nigel agreed. To The Saddle Club he explained, "Beatrice is completely dedicated to competitive riding. Her goal is to win a gold medal in the

Olympics." Nigel shut a tack trunk and sighed. He shook his head. "She has the talent—"

"Talent schmalent," David interrupted. "Lots of people have talent—"

"She has the talent," Nigel repeated, "but only half the attitude."

Stevie was puzzled. "What do you mean?"

"She rides very well and works very hard at it," Nigel explained. "She's willing to do whatever she needs to do in order to win. She rides her horse correctly, she trains hard, and she never does anything that would hurt Southwood or make him less of an athlete. But she isn't emotionally dedicated to the sport. Have you seen how when she's finished riding she just hands Southwood to whoever's available?"

Stevie nodded.

"Would you—would any of you—expect someone else to take care of your horse?"

They all shook their heads. Caring for horses was an important part of riding.

"Beatrice never takes care of Southwood," Nigel said. "She never rides any other horses. A true champion ought to be immersed in horses—ought to think horses, breathe horses, live horses, dream horses—and Beatrice isn't. She wants to be an Olympian. She doesn't want to be a great rider."

Kate came through the door. "Look at me!" she cried. She was wearing white breeches, a yellow vest, and a black shadbelly coat with long tails—formal dressage gear. "Isn't this great?" Kate said. She spun on her heel and the tails of her coat spun around her. "Karen has two—she's letting me use this one—and I've got a body protector and a jersey for cross-country, and a stock tie, and a coat for show jumping. It's perfect!" She shook David's hand. "You've got a very nice wife and I'm pleased to meet you," she said. "Very pleased. Now I have to go take this off before I get dirt on it."

"Put it in the truck!" Nigel called after her.

"I will!" They could hear Kate's quick footsteps hurrying down the aisle.

"That's the attitude you want," David said approvingly.

"Kate's always had a great attitude," Lisa said warmly. "She really loves horses."

"Nigel?" Carole asked. "Where are the Olympics after Atlanta?"

"Sydney, Australia."

Stevie smiled. "What a nice place to visit!"

KATE USED DOROTHY'S bathroom to change into her normal clothes. Back in the living room, she laid her borrowed finery across the sofa. Black coat, yellow vest, string gloves. Kate touched the protective vest with her finger. She had one of her own; she had all of these clothes. She had a dressage saddle, a cross-country saddle, a show-jumping saddle. Somewhere in the hot attic of the Bar None ranch house was a tack trunk, painted with her initials, with all the remnants of her former life inside. Her mother had a scrapbook filled with interviews and photographs of Kate from magazines.

This will be different, she promised herself. Once she had dreamed about becoming an Olympic rider. Kate never minded the hard work, but she had learned that her own attitude turned the dream into something more like a nightmare.

Once, at a preliminary event, the horse that was favored to win had lost a shoe on the cross-country course and pulled up limping. Kate had been glad. Glad because of another horse's misfortune! Glad because with that horse out she had a better chance to win.

At a different event, right before the show-jumping phase, a rider named Amy had asked her a question about the course, and Kate had deliberately given her an incorrect answer. She had lied. Amy went off course and was eliminated, and Kate won. Until that day, Amy had been one of Kate's best friends. Since then Amy hadn't spoken to her. No dream, not even an Olympic one, was worth destroying a friendship the way Kate had.

But this was only one event. Southwood was not her horse. She did not have to win. This would be different, she promised herself. But as she packed Karen's clothing into garment bags, she began to wonder just what would make this event different.

WHILE DOROTHY AND Nigel made a last check of their lists, Drew began to load the horses onto the trailer. Drew had put in Campfire, a bright blood bay, and was just coming around the corner of the trailer when Lisa came out of the stable leading Southwood. Drew jumped, surprised, and walked straight into the corner of the trailer door.

"Oww!" he yelled, falling back. He covered his forehead with his hand. Blood dripped between his fingers.

"Are you okay?" Lisa rushed forward to help him. She tied Southwood to the door of the van and knelt beside Drew. "All I've got are some tissues." She handed him a tissue from the pocket of her sweatshirt.

"Thanks." Drew mopped the cut with it. "How bad does it look?"

Lisa inspected his forehead. "It's bleeding a lot, but it's just a little cut."

"I'll heal, then. Let's take care of Southwood." Together they settled the horse inside the trailer and closed the doors.

"I'm so sorry," Lisa apologized. "I must have startled you. Wait here, I'll get you a Band-Aid." She hurried into the tack room, where she remembered seeing a first aid kit.

"It wasn't your fault," Drew said when she returned. "It was just an accident." He took the Band-Aid from her and smiled, a slightly lopsided smile that matched his lopsided eyebrows. "It's kind of nice getting this chance to talk with you—I'm not very comfortable around people I don't know. I've liked having you girls here today, though. You're my little brother's age—I bet you'd like him a lot. Especially you, Lisa. He'd like you. But he's shy with girls, like me. Not like our older brother!"

"How many brothers and sisters do you have?" Lisa sat down on the bumper of the trailer and listened to Drew describe his large family and his hometown in Maine. He was nice, she decided. A little weird, but nice.

Kate came out of the house with her gear and the rest of The Saddle Club's gear all neatly stowed in their duffel bags. "Is there room for these in the trailer?" she asked Drew.

Drew shook his head. "Sorry. You'll have to stuff them in the truck."

Kate smiled. "Lisa, it's going to be a long drive to the horse trials with you sitting on my lap."

KATE WAS RIGHT. Even though Drew was staying behind to take care of the other horses, Nigel's four-wheel drive was packed. Dorothy had explained that they were going to spend two nights in a hotel to be near the event. The girls had left their sleeping bags behind, but Dorothy's and Nigel's suitcases took their place. They were crammed like pickles in a jar.

· The Saddle Club didn't care. Stevie couldn't remember when she'd been more excited about going to a show that she wasn't actually riding in. This could be the rebirth of Kate's great riding career.

Kate began to talk about other events. "I remember riding endurance day in the rain," she said. "My horse hated rain. We went out to trot the roads and tracks, which is like an official warm-up in a three-day event, and I could hardly see the course markers, and the whole way through my horse kept his tail hunched and his ears flat. He *hated* it."

"You didn't jump cross-country in the rain, did you?" Lisa asked.

"Sure! It was impossible to see. The ground was good, though, and they spread sawdust near the jumps, and the horses wore big cleats on their shoes. Even though my horse hated rain, he loved cross-country, so he did okay. It was the first part I was afraid we weren't going to finish. I thought I'd be the only rider in the history of the world eliminated on road and tracks." Kate laughed. There was a sparkle in her eye that her friends had not seen before.

"Have you ever wanted to go to Australia, Kate?" Lisa asked.

"Sure," Kate said. "Why not?" She looked puzzled when her friends laughed.

58

6

IT WAS LATE afternoon by the time they pulled into the show grounds for the horse trials. Nigel parked the trailer near the temporary stalls, which were set up under a giant tent. Dorothy went to register the horses, and Nigel spoke to an official to learn which stalls belonged to Southwood and Campfire.

"Can I help unload the horses?" Stevie asked, opening the latch at the back of the trailer.

"Not quite yet," Nigel said. "We have to get the stalls ready first. Let's have a look."

They followed him down the dirt aisle to two center stalls. "Kate, you and Stevie check over this stall, and Carole and Lisa can do the other. Look for any nails or splinters that could cut the horses." Nigel went back to the trailer and returned with buckets, feed tubs, and hay nets, which they fastened to the walls of each stall.

Dorothy came back with the numbers Kate and Nigel would wear during competition. She admired the job they'd done preparing the stalls. "You girls work hard," she said. "This goes a lot faster with you here."

Dorothy unloaded the horses. Campfire looked around his stall nervously and whinnied a few times. "He's always like that," Dorothy told Carole. Southwood seemed relaxed. He lipped some hay out of his net and sniffed at his water.

They carried all the tack trunks into the aisle near the horses' stalls. The girls helped Dorothy and Nigel unload.

Finally all their gear was sorted and the horses were comfortable. Nigel found a parking space for his trailer and unhitched it from his truck.

"Whew!" Stevie said, collapsing across the hay bales she'd help stack in the aisle. "I'm so hungry, I could eat a horse trailer! But I'd hate to have to do that—when's dinner?"

Nigel smiled. "You can go get something now, if you like," he said. "Kate and I need to go walk the cross-country course while it's still light enough to see the fences."

Stevie hopped up. "That sounds cool. I guess dinner can wait."

They all went out to walk the fences. The courses were each several miles long, and the fences were huge. "I thought I'd seen a lot of events," Carole said, standing in a ditch and looking up at a fence that towered over her head. "I've never seen fences this big."

"You've never seen an advanced course," Nigel reminded her.

"This fence isn't big," Lisa said, walking over to a small set of barrels. "I could jump this on Prancer."

"That's not an advanced fence," Nigel said. "Cross-country fences are permanent, you know, so they tend to build several courses on the same piece of land. I'll be riding at preliminary level tomorrow, and Kate at advanced, and our courses will cover most of the same ground even though we jump different fences."

Nigel brought Carole back to the giant jump-and-ditch combination she had stood in earlier. "See these wooden flags sticking out from the fence, one on each side? You always keep the white flag on your left. You keep the red flag on your right, no matter what. And see the diamond under the red flag? That shape tells you that this jump is for the advanced course—other levels have other shapes. And the number in the diamond tells you what number fence it is—you jump them in order, one, two, three, four."

"So Kate can tell what fences to jump by reading the flags?" Lisa asked.

"If I have to read the flags, I'm lost," Kate said. "I'll

61

remember the course." She sounded fierce, almost annoyed by Lisa's comment. *Of course*, Lisa thought, with a flash of sympathetic understanding, *Kate's feeling nervous about jumping all these enormous fences.*

They went around the course from jump to jump. Nigel studied the preliminary fences while Dorothy and Kate looked at the advanced ones. At each fence, Kate and Dorothy studied the approach and decided where it was best for Southwood to take off. They talked about how fast he should be traveling when he jumped and how Kate should sit when he landed. They discussed the different ways Kate could ride through some of the complex fences.

It was long and complicated, and it made The Saddle Club feel dizzy. This was too much for anyone to remember! There were more than twenty fences, and Southwood would not get to see them until Kate was asking him to jump them in the actual event. Suddenly The Saddle Club realized how big a move this was for Kate. "Nigel and Beatrice must think a lot of her riding," Carole said as they sat on a fence and watched Kate solemnly pace the approach to it.

"We think a lot of her riding, too," Lisa reminded her.

"Yes, but"—Carole grimaced—"look at this jump! It's made out of giant logs! If Kate doesn't ride it correctly, she could get hurt."

"Kate knows what she's doing," Stevie said. "Besides,

you know as well as I do that people tend to get hurt on horses only when they're in over their heads. Kate can do this. We've seen her do all sorts of stuff at the Bar None, and we saw her ride Giacomo this morning. She can do this." She snapped a photo of Carole and Lisa sitting on the jump.

"I know she can," Carole said. "I know it, but I still worry a little."

"We all do," Lisa replied. "But Kate will be fine."

"What do you think Kate's Olympic course will look like?" Stevie asked.

"Bigger," Carole said promptly. "Scarier, neater, and more exciting!"

"I saw a photograph of the Los Angeles Olympic course once," Lisa said. "The jumps were covered with flowers."

Stevie giggled. "If Kate fell off, she'd have a nice fragrant landing." The others glared at her. "Not that Kate will fall off," Stevie amended hastily.

"No," Lisa said. Her voice took on a dreamy tone. "Can't you just see her standing on the podium, the gold medal around her neck, the American flag waving, and our national anthem being played?"

"I wonder if Kate knows the words," Stevie said.

WHEN THEY FINISHED walking the courses, it was dark. Nigel and Kate went to a competitors' meeting, and the others fed Campfire and Southwood dinner. Nigel came back with the event schedule, which he taped to the outside of Southwood's stall.

"My dressage test is at 8:37 A.M., and I start cross-country at 10:50," he said. "Kate goes later. Her dressage is at 9:52. She begins cross-country at 12:15."

Kate leaned against Southwood's stall. She looked overwhelmed, Carole thought, but not unhappy. Carole went and stood beside her.

"Why don't I take The Saddle Club back to the hotel and check in?" Dorothy suggested. "Then we'll scope out a place for dinner."

"What about Nigel and Kate?" Lisa asked.

"We've got to braid the horses' manes and tails," Kate said quietly. "They have to look sharp for dressage tomorrow."

Lisa nodded. Dorothy had already told them that there was a horse inspection at 6:45 A.M. Campfire and Southwood would need to be ready by then.

"We can help," Carole suggested. "I'm not that good at braiding tails, but I can do manes, and Southwood's looks easy."

"I can do Campfire's mane," Stevie volunteered. "Nigel, you and Kate can do their tails. That way we'll get it done in half the time."

Dorothy put her arm through Lisa's. "We'll get all our

stuff into the hotel rooms and hang Kate's and Nigel's show coats up before they get too wrinkled."

"Great," said Lisa. "Years of unpacking the trunks my mother packed for me have prepared me for this moment. I'm definitely the right person for the job."

IT WAS AFTER nine o'clock that night before Stevie finally slid into the orange plastic booth of a fast-food restaurant near their hotel. "Cheeseburgers!" she groaned. "Give me cheeseburgers!"

"Right away," Nigel said cheerfully, sliding a loaded tray onto the table. They all grabbed at the burgers and fries. "Eat up," he said. "If you finish these I'll buy more. If it hadn't been for you girls, I would still be at the show grounds." He munched a french fry and grinned at Dorothy. "Tell them, Doro," he said.

"Nigel hates braiding manes," Dorothy said promptly. "You girls saved him."

"Dorothy makes me do it," Nigel said, blowing the paper wrapper off his straw at his wife. "She won't help."

"It's good for your soul," Dorothy said.

"Cheeseburgers," said Stevie, "are good for mine."

CAROLE CLOSED THE door of the girls' hotel room. "Dorothy and Nigel say good-night," she said.

Stevie sat up in bed. "Where's Kate?" she asked. "I thought you went to get her."

Carole took off her shoes. "She said she'll be a little while yet. She's going over the dressage test with Nigel. She's got to have it memorized, you know."

"I forgot about that," Stevie said. In dressage, every horse and rider rode a set combination of moves called a test. They received scores from judges based on how accurately, correctly, and beautifully they performed those moves. It was a little bit like the compulsory figures in gymnastics or ice-skating.

"She says we should go to sleep," Carole continued. "She'll be in as soon as she can."

"Poor Kate," Lisa murmured as she drifted off to sleep.

7

BRRRNG! BRRRNG! THE hotel room phone rang in the darkness of night. Lisa fumbled with the receiver, her heart pounding. Who could be calling at this hour?

"Hello?" she asked sleepily.

"This is your requested wake-up call," came the impersonal voice of the front-desk clerk.

"It can't be," Lisa protested. "We just fell asleep." But the clerk had already hung up.

Kate pushed back the covers of the other bed and flipped the bedside lamp on. She shook her head once, as if to clear it, and walked to the bathroom.

"Kate!" Lisa said, watching her. "We don't have to get up yet! It's four in the morning!"

Kate turned and grinned. "I told Nigel we'd all be ready by four-fifteen."

"What do we have to do?" Stevie grumbled. "I thought the whole point of braiding those horses last night was not to have to do it this morning." She began to get dressed.

"Well, Southwood and Campfire need to eat an early breakfast," Carole said. "You know it's not good for horses to work hard right after they've eaten."

"Sure, but . . . ," Stevie said. She held up a pair of blue jeans. "Are these yours, Carole, or mine?"

Lisa grabbed them. "Mine, I think. See the hole in the pocket? Southwood's going to have to be groomed, too. We don't want him covered with hay for the horse inspection."

Kate came back. "Bathroom's free," she said. "You guys are right. We need to take care of Southwood early. Also, Nigel promised to walk the course with me again before he has to get ready." Kate shuddered, and her friends were reminded of all the big fences that awaited her and Southwood. "I can't decide on the best way to ride through the water complex," Kate said.

"Poor Kate," Lisa said sympathetically. "Did you dream about the cross-country fences?"

Kate laughed. "Dream? No! To dream I would have had to sleep. I just lay there and worried about them!"

Carole looked up in amazement. "Are you really afraid?" she asked. "If you are, Kate, I don't think you should do this. Nigel could ride Southwood. Beatrice would understand."

Kate smiled, but without humor. "I don't think Beatrice would understand, Carole, but it doesn't matter because I'm not afraid. I promise. I have a nice, healthy respect for those fences, but I know Southwood and I can manage them. I never could sleep before a competition. I always get this way."

"But this is just for fun," Lisa reminded her.

Kate gave her the same tight-lipped smile. "Nothing this big is entirely for fun. At least, it isn't for me."

"You need to put this in perspective," Stevie suggested. "Compared to a lot of other competitions, this is pretty small."

Kate laughed. "Small compared to what? The world championships?"

"Or the Olympics," Lisa said seriously, with a nod of her head. "This is definitely small compared to the Olympics."

"Okay," Kate said. She was smiling now, and she definitely looked more relaxed. "When I'm galloping up to that giant log pile on the course I'll just say to myself, 'That's nothing—in the Olympics they have much bigger fences.' That'll sure make me feel better."

THE STABLES WERE lit by rows of bright yellow lightbulbs. In the early morning darkness, the lights and the stable tent combined to give the event a carnival atmosphere. All the riders were there early. The Saddle Club helped feed Campfire and Southwood, then began to clean their stalls while Kate groomed Southwood.

Stevie hauled a muck bucket into Campfire's stall. "Oh, say, can you see-e-e," she began to sing as she forked old bedding into the bucket, "by-y the dawn's ear-ly light—"

"Stevie!" Lisa covered her ears.

"C'mon, sing along," Stevie urged her. "We need to make sure Kate knows the words!"

Reluctantly, Lisa agreed. "Start over," she said.

This time the effect was worse. Lisa was a much better singer than Stevie, but her voice only seemed to emphasize how off Stevie's was. "Hey, in there!" Kate shouted. "Knock it off! You're frightening Southwood!"

"Sing along, Kate!" Stevie said. "That way he'll know there's nothing to be afraid off!"

Kate poked her head into Campfire's stall. "What gave you the urge to sing so early in the morning, anyway?"

"Patriotism!" Stevie replied with a grin. Carole came out of Southwood's stall and laughed. All four girls burst into song. "Oh, say, can you se-e-e—"

"Honestly!" Nigel walked into the aisle, shaking his head in indignation. "I'm surrounded by Yanks!" He stopped, put his hand over his heart, and began to sing "God Save the Queen" loudly enough to drown the rest of them out. Nigel ended triumphantly, ". . . *God save the*

Queen!" just as the rest of them hit ". . . home of the *brave!*" They looked at one another solemnly for a long moment, and then burst out laughing.

"Now we know she knows the words," Stevie whispered to Lisa with satisfaction as they returned to their pitchforks and bucket. "That's one big step toward winning an international competition!" They giggled at Stevie's silliness.

HORSE INSPECTION TOOK place on a stretch of asphalt road near the dressage ring. Carole knew that the horses were being watched for signs of lameness or illness that would indicate they shouldn't compete that day. Kate trotted Southwood up and back across the asphalt, then held him while he was briefly examined by a veterinarian. Southwood passed with flying colors. "Unless a horse gets injured trailering here," Dorothy explained, "there's almost no chance he'll fail the first inspection. The important inspection comes tomorrow, after cross-country."

As soon as their horses completed the inspection, Kate and Nigel left to walk the cross-country course one last time. Dorothy looked at Southwood and Campfire. "Well," she suggested to The Saddle Club, "it might help these two to graze a little. It would relax them. Could you guys find them a quiet spot with some nice grass?"

"We'd love to," they said. Stevie found a spot close to the stabling yet secluded from the bustle around the dressage ring. Carole and Lisa led the horses to it.

"Do you think Kate is catching the Olympic spirit?" Carole asked.

"It's hard to tell," Lisa answered. "I think we'll know better after we watch her jump the cross-country course. But she's really working hard at this competition, and I think that's a good sign."

Stevie leaned against Southwood's flank. "We need to start thinking about where to get an Olympic horse for Kate."

"Well . . ." Lisa paused. "I know Olympic horses are special, but the Devines already have so many horses at the Bar None. Do you think one of them might work?"

"Stewball," Stevie said instantly. "He's the smartest." When her friends laughed, she added, "Oh, all right, I know he won't work. We've been through that before!" At one point, before Stevie got Belle, she'd almost bought Stewball and taken him home to Pine Hollow. Lisa, Carole, and Kate had helped Stevie see that Stewball was much happier as a cow pony than he would have been under English saddle.

"Maybe Moonglow," Carole suggested. Moonglow was a mare Kate had adopted from a wild herd. "She's really done well in her training so far."

"But could she ever be as athletic as Southwood?" Stevie argued. "Or as smart as Stewball?"

Carole shrugged. "You never know until you try. Think

about how it would sound: 'Next on course for the United States, Katharine Devine and Moonglow!' "

"Like poetry," Lisa said, and the others agreed.

"That's enough grass," Carole said a few minutes later, checking her watch. "We need to start tacking up Campfire now. Nigel needs to warm him up before they do their dressage."

They returned to the stables. Dorothy settled Nigel's heavy dressage saddle across Campfire's withers, and then the show PA system squawked and hissed and spat out Dorothy's name. "Dorothy DeSoto, please come to the main office," it said. "You have a phone call."

"Drew!" Dorothy said, and hurried away.

"He's probably the only person who knows the show's phone number," Stevie said thoughtfully. She adjusted Campfire's saddle and buckled the girth on one side. "I hope none of the other horses are sick."

They worked in worried silence until Dorothy returned. Her pale face seemed to confirm The Saddle Club's fear. "Is it Warrior?" Carole asked.

Dorothy sank down on a hay bale. "Worse than that," she whispered. "It's Beatrice. She's had an accident. She may never ride again."

8

THE SADDLE CLUB clustered around Dorothy. "What happened?" Stevie asked.

Dorothy blew out a long breath. "That was Drew on the phone," she said. "He told me Beatrice met her family in Saint Croix yesterday afternoon. Last night they all went out for a moonlight boat ride. Beatrice dived off the bow of the boat and hit a reef just beneath the water's surface."

Dorothy shuddered. "She fractured her skull, but they think she'll be okay. She's in surgery this morning. Beatrice's father called to tell us about the accident. It certainly sounds as if she won't be coming back. I imagine Southwood will be sold."

"But you said they think she'll be okay," Lisa said. "Why

would she have to give up Southwood? She could still ride."

"Maybe." Dorothy shrugged. "I don't have the whole story yet—I just know what Drew told me. But if Beatrice's injuries are as severe as they sound, I doubt she'll ride again. It'll be a long time before she's allowed to get back on a horse, and she'd have to work extremely hard to regain her skill. She'd have to really love riding in order to do that."

"Doesn't she love riding?" Carole asked softly.

Dorothy looked at her. "What do you think?"

Carole bit her lip, then shook her head sadly. Beatrice loved to be successful. She loved to win. She never seemed to truly love riding.

"She'll never be content to ride without winning," Dorothy said. "And it would be a long time, if ever, before she wins again. I'd say this is the end of Beatrice's riding career."

The Saddle Club had all seen the accident that ended Dorothy's riding career. "When you got hurt, you didn't give up horses," Lisa reminded Dorothy.

Dorothy smiled. "That's because I love them more than anything," she said. "I can't imagine doing anything else with my life. I'm very lucky, because even though I can't ride I'm still healthy and I can train students and work with horses. Being married to Nigel keeps me involved in competition, too.

"Beatrice's accident sounds more serious in the short run, and less serious in the long run, than mine. When I was hurt it wasn't very long before I could leave the hospital, but the doctors told me not to ride again. It sounds like Beatrice will be able to recover fully, but it might take her a long time. But Beatrice and I are very different in what our goals are and in what makes us happy. Anything I can do with horses makes me happy."

This made perfect sense to The Saddle Club. None of them could imagine Beatrice struggling to regain her riding skills. She had never struggled for anything.

"Beatrice's father told Drew that she had sent us one message," Dorothy said thoughtfully. "She asked us to please take good care of Southwood. It's the last thing she said before they took her into surgery."

The Saddle Club was silent for a moment. Carole reflected that that was the first nonbratty thing she had ever heard of Beatrice saying. "Maybe she loves Southwood after all," Carole said.

"Maybe she does," Dorothy agreed. "I wouldn't have said so before. I thought she only saw him as a means to an end."

Dorothy wiped her hand across her face, then stood. "We still need to get this horse ready for Nigel," she said, patting Campfire on the neck. "I have a favor to ask you girls. I'll tell Nigel about Beatrice as soon as I can, but I'd

76

rather Kate didn't know right away. She's got enough to think about today with her cross-country round. Can you keep a secret? Just for now. We'll tell her soon."

The Saddle Club agreed. They wanted Kate to be able to focus on her ride.

WHEN KATE AND Nigel returned from the course, The Saddle Club realized that Kate was already completely focused on her ride. She hardly seemed to see her friends.

"Here, Kate," Lisa called. "We've got Southwood all tacked up for you. Look how handsome he is!"

Kate took Southwood's reins without even glancing at Lisa. "Great," she said briskly. "Nigel! Where can I ride him?"

Nigel was fussing over Campfire, checking his tack and making small adjustments. "I'm going to the warm-up dressage arena," he said. "I want good smooth footing for a real warm-up, but you don't need that yet and the arena's going to be crowded. Why don't you head for the field next to the show-jumping ring? Just ride him for a little while, gently, and get to know him. No fancy moves, not yet.

"When they start the advanced-level dressage, go up to the ring and watch the first few tests. Then I'll come back and help you with his real warm-up."

Kate nodded. "Okay." She checked her girth, mounted Southwood, and rode off without a backward glance.

"Hold Campfire for a moment, won't you, Carole?" Nigel said. "Dorothy! Where's my top hat?" Nigel rummaged through a trunk.

"Where did you put it?" Dorothy asked calmly. She found the hat and set it on Nigel's head. He took it off, frowned quizzically at Dorothy, and disappeared into Campfire's stall with an armful of clothes.

"Hey, boy," Carole murmured to Campfire. The horse, though alert, did not seem troubled by the uproar. Carole was not troubled, either, but she did feel a little lost. The news about Beatrice had upset her, and neither Kate nor Nigel seemed like their usual selves.

"Heigh-ho," Nigel said, coming out of the stall. He had used it as a dressing room and was now transformed. Carole laughed. She had seen Nigel dressed in formal dressage gear once before, at an event in England, but it still surprised her to see him looking so dapper. Nigel's black coat was long and elegant, with tails. He wore a white stock tie and white breeches, and his black boots were polished to perfection. Best of all was the genuine top hat on his head.

"You look like you're going to the opera," Lisa said admiringly.

"I hope I don't ride like I'm going to the opera," Nigel replied. "Dorothy!"

"You've got over half an hour," Dorothy said soothingly. "Plenty of time. Relax."

"Good." Nigel took Campfire out of the stable,

78

mounted, and rode off with an expression of fierce concentration.

"He isn't always quite like this," Dorothy said, watching him go with a thoughtful expression. "Nigel hasn't said so to you, but this is an important event for Campfire. It'll tell us a lot about how good he can be."

"Nigel's just so *busy*," Stevie said. "I didn't expect it."

"Yes. Well." Dorothy smiled. "Despite the fact that Kate needs coaching, Nigel isn't really all that busy. Imagine riding several horses and having three or four of your students ride, too. That's what our spring events are like. Of course, Drew comes with us then. Why don't you girls head for the dressage ring? The competition's going to start soon. I have to put together a grooming bucket to take to the ring, but I'll be there in a minute."

The Saddle Club walked off together. They could see a small crowd of people gathering at the dressage ring. Beyond that, a larger crowd of riders worked their horses in the warm-up ring. "I don't see Kate," Stevie said. She stood on her toes, craning to see around a very large horse who was blocking the way. "Didn't Nigel say near the show-jumping arena?"

"There's the arena," Carole said. They dodged their way through the people and horses until they reached the fence surrounding the arena. Empty bleachers stood on both sides.

"There she is," Lisa said, pointing at a lone horse and

rider who were cantering slowly in the deep grass of an adjoining field. Even from a distance, they could tell that Kate's position was beautifully correct and that Southwood was listening to her and responding well. "They look great," Lisa said, "but lonely." She corrected herself. "I mean, alone. Not lonely." But as she looked at Kate, she realized that "lonely" was exactly the right word. Kate seemed isolated, in her own world.

Carole sighed. "I feel a little lonely myself," she said. "I didn't expect this to be such a big deal. Riding is hard work." The thought surprised her. It was certainly never one she'd had before. She looked up at her friends, a half-frightened look on her face.

"No, it isn't," Stevie said firmly. She put a reassuring arm around her. "Showing is hard work. Riding is hard, if you want to do it right, but it's not work. It's the most wonderful fun you can have—especially when you do it with friends!"

Carole felt much better.

IN THE CENTER of the dressage arena, a woman on a sleek brown Thoroughbred drew to a square halt. She paused, her horse's neck finely arched to the bit, then let the reins run loose through her fingers. She gave the horse a pat, and he stretched his neck long and walked out of the arena.

"Ohhh," Stevie breathed. "That was beautiful. Did you see her extended trots? That horse—"

"Shhh," Lisa said, sitting up straight to see over the people in front of them in the stands. "Here comes Kate."

The Saddle Club watched, mesmerized, as their friend rode into the arena. They had already seen Nigel ride a clean, precise, preliminary-level test, and they knew he was pleased. They had also seen enough of the advanced-level tests to know how good Kate and Southwood needed to be: *very* good.

"Is that really Kate?" Carole murmured. It was hard to recognize their friend in the championship rider they saw entering the ring.

Kate halted and dipped her head for her opening salute. From the halt she sent Southwood into a brisk working trot, and from there she rode the same pattern as all the other advanced-level riders: collections and extensions, trots and canters, tight circles and serpentines. Southwood's movements seemed to flow one into another. His body bent and straightened to Kate's nearly invisible commands. For the finish, Kate brought him to a four-square halt just as the previous rider had, dropped her reins, and gave him a pat. The Saddle Club cheered.

"She looked so *professional,*" Stevie said. The girls clambered down from the spectator stands and went to find their friend. "When we're at the Bar None, she's the only person who dresses more casually than me—scruffy jeans, old cowboy boots. In that ring, she looked like a whole different person!" Stevie waved her camera. "I'm glad I got some pictures of her."

"It wasn't just her clothes, it was her attitude," Lisa said. "Imagine how hard it would be to ride Southwood that well when she doesn't really know him. But Kate just knew she could do it. She's got so much confidence. It's as if the whole thing has to do with confidence, and Kate has it."

By this time they had reached the edge of the arena. Kate and Southwood were halted near the gate, talking to Nigel. To The Saddle Club's surprise, Kate was laughing.

"When I got to the far corner after the first serpentine," she was saying, "I couldn't remember what came next! I knew it was something canter, but I didn't know if it was the counter-canter or the canter pirouette! So I just picked one and hoped for the best." She laughed again. "I thought we were history. I kept waiting for the judges to tell me to try again."

"Kate, you were great!" Stevie said, giving Southwood a pat.

"You looked so cool. I don't think I could have kept my head like that!" Carole added.

"I'm used to it," Kate said. "We could have been better with our collections; we'll be marked down for that. And the fourth loop of the second serpentine stunk. But we didn't have any major errors. Southwood's a good mover."

"He was fantastic!" Stevie said, a little taken aback by Kate's comments. Stevie hadn't seen any of the errors Kate was talking about, and dressage was her specialty. "I'd be thrilled if Belle could ever move so well."

"He was bred to move well," Kate pointed out. "And he is doing well—Nigel and Beatrice are good trainers—but he isn't using his back as well as he could. He needs to round a bit." She sighed. "He's got a nice temperament, and that certainly helps. He didn't fight me."

Carole and Stevie exchanged glances. Even though Stevie loved dressage and Carole knew all about riding, neither of them had ever been quite so picky, or so unemotional, about any performance their horses gave. "So how well did Southwood actually do?" Stevie asked at last.

"I'd guess we'll end up in the middle of the pack," Kate said. "That still puts us in contention to win. We weren't brilliant, but we didn't have any big goof ups. The hardest part comes next."

Kate began walking Southwood back to the stables, and the rest of The Saddle Club trailed behind her. Suddenly Kate halted Southwood. "Look," she said quietly. She used her dressage whip to point to a gray horse and female rider who were warming up for their dressage test.

"It's Karen!" Lisa said, recognizing Dorothy's friend. "Gosh, what a beautiful horse!" She waved, and Karen, who was close enough to hear them, nodded back and smiled.

"Too bad her horse isn't traveling straight," Kate said, in a louder voice.

"Kate, what are you talking about? He looks perfectly straight!" Stevie was astonished.

"No, he's not, and he's not using his hind end at all," Kate continued, still loud enough for Karen to hear every word.

"Kate, shhh! She'll hear you!" Carole hissed.

Kate looked at Karen for a moment longer, and then

down at her friends. They were shocked by the dark expression on her face. "That should give her something to think about," Kate said, more quietly. "Right before her test, too." She sounded satisfied.

"But Kate! She's a friend!" Lisa could hardly believe that Kate would do such a thing—deliberately try to upset Karen right before her competition.

Kate's look of satisfaction faded as she saw The Saddle Club's dismay. She dropped her eyes as if ashamed. "There are no friends in competition," she said at last.

"But of course there are!" Carole protested.

"I never found any," Kate snapped back. She did feel ashamed. Already her old problems were coming back! Why was it never enough for her to do her best? Why did she have to beat everyone else? She didn't know. She only knew that something about competition made her heart turn sour. They returned to the stables in silence.

WHILE THEY WERE still in Southwood's stall taking off his dressage gear, Dorothy came down the aisle. She had a big smile on her face and a piece of paper in her hands. "They just posted the dressage results," she said. "Kate, out of thirty-three riders, you're in eighth place!"

Kate's eyes shone bright. "We did better than I thought, then," she said. She started to bend down to take off one of Southwood's leg wraps, but Dorothy caught her into a hug.

"Do you realize how good that is?" Dorothy asked. "You were fantastic! Everyone's been talking about you."

Kate gave Dorothy a small fierce smile. "Great," she said. She bent down again, finished removing the wrap, and stood back up. "Where did Karen place?" she asked.

Dorothy checked. "She's got two horses in your division," she said. "Her young one must have had a problem—he's twenty-seventh. Her old veteran, Singalong, is fifth."

"What color is her old horse, Singalong?" Carole asked softly.

"Gray. Her young horse is a bay."

Carole nodded, feeling relieved. At least Kate's comment hadn't caused Karen to ride poorly.

Kate nodded, too. "I think I'll go check out the competition. I won't be long." She pushed past the rest of The Saddle Club and left the stabling area.

"Whoa." Lisa watched Kate walk away. "That was weird. She didn't give us a chance to congratulate her. And why would she say those things about Karen's horse, back when we were by the dressage arena? That was really rude!"

"What things?" Dorothy asked. With some hesitation, Lisa and Carole described what Kate had said.

"The horse was doing fine," Stevie added. "I think Kate just wanted Karen to mess up."

Dorothy nodded, looking sad. "It's a common enough

technique—trying to make your opponent nervous. I'm sorry that Kate sank to doing it, but I wouldn't worry about it too much. Karen's far too experienced to be bothered by anything Kate says, and I'm sure Kate only said it because she's nervous. This is a tough competition for her."

"We know that," Carole said. "It just isn't like her."

"Kate'll be okay," Dorothy assured them. "Now, I'm going to go get sandwiches for all of us. If you see Nigel, tell him so, please. You girls should take a few minutes' rest. You've worked hard this morning."

The Saddle Club sat down on some hay bales. "What a morning," Stevie said, shaking her head. "Kate in eighth place! That's wonderful. After the way she criticized her round, I didn't expect her to do well at all."

"She said she did pretty well," Lisa said. "She seemed satisfied."

"She thought she'd gotten a lot of things wrong, too," Stevie argued. "She mostly talked about the faults they had."

"Well, she's not in first place," Carole answered. "I think Kate critiqued her round fairly. Probably even the first place round wasn't perfect. We're just not used to the standards of this level of competition. But I want to ask you two . . ." Carole picked at a piece of baling twine. "Do you agree with Dorothy? Do you think Kate's attitude is okay, or at least not that big of a deal?"

Stevie heard the unhappiness in Carole's voice. "Do you

mean the way she wants to win at any cost?" she asked. "I know that attitude too well. And I don't think it's okay. I've learned how destructive it can be." Stevie's natural competitiveness had almost caused her to break up with her boyfriend and had once caused her a lot of problems with her horse.

"Maybe it's part of being a top rider," Lisa said tentatively. "At this level, I think you need to be competitive. All of the top riders probably have big goals. Like the Olympics."

Carole shook her head. "I don't think you have to act like Kate just did. Nigel never would, neither would Dorothy."

"Beatrice might," Stevie said.

"Exactly," Carole retorted.

"Well, Beatrice isn't going to the Olympics now. She ought to sell Southwood to Kate." Stevie said the words casually, but the moment they were out of her mouth she recognized them for the brilliant idea they were. Lisa and Carole stared at her open-mouthed.

"They get along so well together," Lisa said.

Carole clapped her hands. "Stevie, you're right! Southwood would be the perfect horse to take Kate to the Olympics!" She smiled at Stevie and Lisa, her unhappiness at Kate's attitude temporarily forgotten. "Maybe it really will happen: our friend, Kate Devine, a gold medal rider!"

10

THE GIRLS STARED at each other with faces full of excited delight. "Well," Stevie said, breaking the slight silence, "I don't think we should tell her our plan right away."

"Right," Lisa agreed. "Kate doesn't know about Beatrice yet anyway. Once she learns that, we can tell her about our plan for the Olympics."

"She'll be thrilled," Carole predicted. "She and Southwood are a great match already. And her parents have so much room at the Bar None, they'll never mind her getting another horse."

Stevie leaned back against the wall of Campfire's stall. "I bet Kate has already thought about it," she said. "The

Olympics, I mean. I bet that's the reason she's taking this so seriously. If she does well here, with no preparation, won't that prove how really great she can be? I bet she's already planning on coming back to competition. With four and a half years' training and the right horse, she could be one of the best in the world."

"Then we can all go to Australia and watch Kate ride," Lisa said dreamily.

Carole smiled. "Watch her and Southwood. He is definitely the right horse."

Nigel came bustling into the barn. He had changed from his dressage gear into a protective vest and a bright green-and-blue jersey. His helmet was covered with matching green-and-blue fabric. "What ho, lazybones!" he cried when he saw The Saddle Club sitting down. "Get up, get up! As you Yanks say, Time's a-wastin'! Where's Doro?"

"Gone to get lunch," Carole said. They scrambled up and helped Nigel bring Campfire out to the cross-ties.

"She must be joking," Nigel declared. "She knows I could never eat right now. Help me get this horse ready, girls!"

They helped saddle and bridle Campfire. The horse let out a loud whinny. From a neighboring aisle, another horse replied.

"Campfire knows it's time for cross-country," Nigel said. "He's ready to run." Nigel sounded pleased.

Dorothy came in with a huge bag of sandwiches and

several sodas. "Sorry I'm so late—the lines were awful! Here, honey, have a sandwich."

Nigel looked at her dolefully. "You can't be serious." He quickly unwrapped a sandwich and took two huge bites.

"Well, then at least have a soda," Dorothy said, grinning at The Saddle Club.

"No, I really can't," Nigel said. He took one and swallowed several gulps. "Thank you. Let's go!"

Nigel buckled his helmet on and picked up his crop. He tied his number around his waist. Dorothy went over Campfire briefly, checking to make sure every buckle of his tack was secure. She kissed Campfire on the nose for luck. She tried to kiss Nigel, but he wouldn't let her. He grabbed Campfire's reins and headed for the start box. The others followed at a slight distance. Stevie took a picture of Nigel mounting.

"Campfire is his baby," Dorothy said. "Nigel raised him from a foal. I hope that horse goes well today."

"How'd they do in dressage?" Stevie asked.

"That's right, I never told you. Top half of the field. Good, for a young horse. We're pleased." Dorothy smiled. "We don't think Campfire's going to be the superstar that Southwood might be, but we think he'll be an advanced horse. He may surprise us, for good or for bad. Today we just want him to jump clear and be brave."

By the time they caught up with him, Nigel was riding Campfire into the open square that was the start box.

91

"He's facing the wrong way!" Lisa said when Nigel made no move to turn his horse.

Dorothy smiled. "Just watch."

A timing official began counting down from ten. Nigel sat poised and ready. Campfire quivered with excitement. "Three! Two! One!" said the announcer. On "One!" Nigel whirled Campfire around. They bolted out of the box at a gallop.

"Oh," said Lisa.

"They always start that way," Dorothy said. "Otherwise, the horse might take off too soon. I'm going to the water complex now. I want to see how Campfire handles himself there."

"We're going up to that big hill," Stevie said, pointing. "We figured out that we can see the entire end of the course from there."

"We'd better hurry," Carole added, catching Stevie by the arm. They waved to Dorothy and took off in the opposite direction. They made it to the top of the large hill before Nigel came into view.

"There he is!" Lisa said. Nigel's green-and-blue shirt shone bright against the winter-brown grass. From far away both he and Campfire looked very small. The jumps still looked big. The Saddle Club held their breath as Campfire cantered up to a big ditch with a log on the edge of it and flew over it like a bird.

"That's amazing," Stevie said. "And Southwood's fences

are even bigger than that!" She raised her camera and snapped a quick picture of Campfire approaching another jump.

Nigel and Campfire took the last three fences well. As they landed after the final fence, The Saddle Club ran down the hill to meet them. By the time they reached Nigel, he was already on the ground, removing Campfire's tack.

Campfire was covered in sweat and breathing hard, but he didn't seem distressed. Nigel, on the other hand, looked completely exhausted. His jersey was soaked with his own sweat, and when he took his helmet off his hair was sopping. He started to unbuckle Campfire's bridle. Lisa saw his fingers tremble.

"Are you okay?" she asked. "Did you hurt yourself?"

Nigel laughed. "I feel like an old man," he said. "No, Lisa, I'm fine. I just had to work very hard to keep Campfire under control out there. He wanted to run as fast as he could. He didn't want to listen when I asked him to slow down."

Dorothy looked over, smiling softly. "Full of himself, was he?" she asked.

"You bet," Nigel replied. "He's a goer." From the looks Dorothy and Nigel exchanged, Carole knew they weren't displeased. Campfire had proved himself brave.

Carole still had half her soda left. She offered it to Nigel, who drained it gratefully. "What if you'd gone too fast?"

she asked. "Would you have gotten penalty points?" She knew that horses were penalized for going too slow.

"No," Nigel said, "but we probably would have run into the fences. Horses can't jump well when they're going that fast. At Campfire's level, he can go pretty slowly and still be within time. Kate, though, is going to have to gallop fast and then slow down for the fences." He frowned. "I'm a little worried that she doesn't know how fast she has to go. Where is Kate, anyway?"

"Looking at the fences," Stevie answered.

"Here I am," said Kate, walking up. "Nice job, Nigel. I saw some of it."

Nigel thanked her. He asked if she knew the time allowed for her course.

"Of course," Kate replied. "Five hundred seventy meters per minute. But I've never had to ride that fast before, so I don't know what it feels like. Will it help if I watch some of the first advanced riders go?"

"Maybe," Nigel said. "I can watch them with you."

"You can borrow my watch," Dorothy offered. "It's got a timer, and you can use it to gauge your speed. I'll show you how."

"I know how," Kate said, taking the watch from her. "I've just never ridden the advanced speed before."

Kate talked a few minutes more with Dorothy, planning her round, and then walked off with Nigel, deep in conversation. Dorothy walked Campfire off to cool him down.

Suddenly The Saddle Club was alone. Kate had come and gone and not said a single word to them.

"Well," Carole said, "I'm sure Kate would have more time to chat if she were used to all this. Picking up a last-minute ride like she did, she has a lot of things to learn right way."

"Of course," Stevie said. "It's been a long time since she's done this."

Lisa stooped to pick up the water bucket Dorothy had brought out for Campfire. "I'm not so sure," she said, a trifle unhappily. "I think maybe top-level riding really does take this kind of huge commitment from the riders. If Kate did this all the time, it would matter an awful lot to her, so I think she would still be this intense. And Dorothy said this was easy, compared to other events."

They began to walk slowly back to the stables, each lost in her own thoughts.

"Being intense is one thing," Stevie said. "I mean, Kate was almost rude to Dorothy back there, but I know she didn't mean to be. On the other hand, she was rude to Karen on purpose. That wasn't right."

"Kate has a long time before the Olympics. She can work on her attitude, too," suggested Carole. "The Olympics—just think about it! They're a dream come true. A trip to the Olympics would be worth almost anything."

"Of course it would be," Lisa said. "But Kate's going to have to work really hard."

"We can help her," Stevie said firmly. "We'll be her Olympic support crew. Right now, we can start by getting Southwood ready for cross-country."

In his stall, Southwood was munching hay. He seemed excited but happy, and he nickered when he saw them.

"You know," Stevie said as they put Southwood's halter on and tied him in the aisle, "before we were comparing Kate's riding to Beatrice's, but I think it's obvious that Kate's a much better horsewoman than Beatrice. She took her time warming Southwood up for dressage this morning, and she spent a long time taking care of him afterward. Kate's not like Beatrice. Kate really cares about her horses."

"Nigel said that Beatrice's biggest problem was her attitude," Lisa pointed out. "Kate's attitude toward Southwood is great. She loves doing everything with horses. Imagine Beatrice riding bareback the way Kate does at the ranch! The only thing Kate needs to work on is her attitude toward other riders, and I know we can help her with that!"

Carole began to brush the dust off Southwood's gleaming coat. "It's going to be so exciting when Kate goes to the Olympics!" she said. "I can hardly wait! Do you think we'll be able to go?"

"We could help groom," Stevie said. "I bet Kate would let us."

96

"I'm just sure she'll make it," Lisa said. "She's almost a perfect horsewoman." Lisa grinned. "We should start saving for our tickets, don't you think?"

Stevie caught on right away. "Our plane tickets to Sydney, Australia? I think we should fly first-class!"

11

CAROLE WATCHED AS Kate and Southwood waited in the start box. Kate's mouth was set in a tense grim line. Southwood's nostrils quivered with excitement. "Three!" the starter called. Kate sat forward slightly and Carole saw her legs tighten against Southwood's sides. "Two!" Southwood tossed his head. "One!" Kate and Southwood whirled in a single movement and galloped onto the course.

"Go, Kate!" Carole screamed. She clutched Stevie's and Lisa's arms. They watched Southwood take the first fence of the advanced course. Kate had called it easy, but it was nearly four feet high! Southwood cleared it effortlessly, flicking his tail in the air as he jumped.

As soon as he landed safely, the girls started to run

98

toward the hill from which they'd watched Nigel's ride. "Hey!" Nigel called. "You can't see Kate's course well from there. Follow me, I know a good spot!" They turned and hurried to catch up with him and Dorothy.

From their new vantage point they could see three jumps. Not bad, Carole decided, considering that the course was more than four miles long.

The first jump was a broken bridge—a wooden structure jutting out into space. As Kate approached, Lisa could hardly bear to watch. This fence seemed worse to her than all the others.

Kate didn't hesitate at all. Nor did Southwood. They galloped down the slope to the bridge, trotted across the wooden span, then leaped off the end of it into open air. It was nearly six feet down. They landed galloping. Through the viewfinder of her camera Stevie saw Kate's hand go up briefly to stroke Southwood's neck.

"Oh my," Lisa whispered with pride.

The second fence was shaped like a giant picnic table. "That looks bigger than the one we have in our backyard at home," Stevie said.

"It should," Nigel replied. "It's eight feet wide at the bottom."

"They won't go all the way over it, will they?" Carole asked. "Can Southwood land on top and jump off?"

"He could," Dorothy said. "The fence is strong enough, if he tries to."

"That's what I'd do," Stevie said. Nigel grinned. Kate and Southwood galloped toward the table. This time, instead of slowing him, Kate let him gallop on. They cleared the table in one fluid, massive leap.

"Oh my!" Lisa said again, this time feeling her heart in her throat.

"Wow!" Stevie cried.

"Go, Kate!"

The third jump was made of both logs and hedges, and it led into a wood. After Kate and Southwood soared over it, they were hidden from The Saddle Club's sight. The girls stared at the fence for a moment after Kate was gone. She was marvelous.

"Olympic material, all the way," Stevie said slowly. Lisa and Carole nodded.

"What's that?" Dorothy asked. She turned toward them with a puzzled smile. Nigel also looked curious.

"We were thinking how great it would be if Kate bought Southwood," Lisa explained. "She could take Beatrice's place and train him for the Olympics."

"I see," Dorothy said. She nodded her head as if she understood.

"Kate could do it, don't you think?" asked Lisa.

Dorothy looked at Nigel. He put a thoughtful hand to his chin. "We'd better start walking back," he suggested. "We want to be there when Kate comes in.

"Dorothy told me about Beatrice," Nigel continued. "In fact, right before Kate started I went to the show office and called Saint Croix for an update. Beatrice's surgery went well, and they do expect her to recover fully in time. However, everyone, including Beatrice, her family, and me, doubts that she'll return to riding. So yes, if Kate wants to buy Southwood, I imagine that she could. If Kate wants to be a top rider again, she could work toward that, too. Did she say she wants to?"

"We haven't asked her yet," Lisa admitted. "But Kate and Southwood make such a fabulous pair—they're both so talented—we're sure they could do it!"

"A horse like Southwood is very expensive," Dorothy commented. "Training is expensive, too."

"We know that," Stevie said. "But maybe Kate's parents could sell some of their other horses and get Southwood instead. I bet they would."

"Kate wouldn't be able to live at the Bar None," Nigel said. "She'd be too far away from other horse trainers and from the events she'd need to compete at."

"We talked about that, too, while Kate was heading down to the start," Carole said. "We figure she could come live with me and my dad and train at Pine Hollow the way you did, Dorothy."

Dorothy smiled. "Max is a great trainer, but after I reached a certain point I needed to learn from people who only did eventing," she said. "I think it would be the same for Kate. However, she could move in with me and Nigel. She could live with us, work for us, and train with us."

"That'd be perfect!" Carole said. The others agreed. If they were lucky, they'd be able to visit Kate a lot. She wouldn't be so far away.

"Of course, Kate still has school," Nigel commented. "She'd have to work with Southwood, and at the barn, several hours a day, study at night, and go to events on weekends. It would be hard."

"She doesn't mind hard work," Lisa said. "You know that."

"She'd have to give up all the fun things she does on the ranch, as well as everything else in her normal life," Nigel said. "She'd have to be thoroughly devoted to riding. Of course, many people are—some of them even younger than Kate."

"Even the most talented and dedicated riders don't necessarily make the Olympic team," Dorothy added. "You have to have the right horse at the right time. If you or your horse gets injured, or if your horse is too old or too young, or you just have a bad year, you won't make it. I think if Kate wants to make riding her life, Nigel and I are all for it, but I don't think the Olympics should be her only goal."

Carole frowned. "It was Beatrice's only goal." They stopped and watched another competitor gallop past before ducking under the ropes that marked the course. The finish line was in sight. Kate would be there soon.

"Exactly." Nigel smiled. "And what did you all think of Beatrice?"

The Saddle Club was silent for a moment. "Kate is nothing like Beatrice," Stevie said hotly.

"No," Dorothy agreed, in a gentle voice. "She's not."

"Plenty of riders have talent," Nigel said, "even Kate's level of talent, but not too many have the sort of drive that it takes to be a champion. An Olympic rider needs to be everything at the same time—talented, dedicated, hard-working, and lucky." He laughed a short laugh. "Maybe that's why there aren't so many of them."

A horse and rider galloped over the crest of a small rise in front of them and headed for the finish. "That's Kate!" Lisa cried. They ran after her.

Kate pulled Southwood up with a look of triumph on her face. She patted him briefly before vaulting off his back and undoing the girth of his saddle. The rest of The Saddle Club hurried to help. Dorothy had brought supplies right to the finish line so they would be able to take care of Southwood immediately. Lisa held Southwood and patted him, Carole slipped a cooling sheet over his back, and Stevie began to sponge his legs and neck with water. Southwood was lathered and breathing hard, but he looked magnificent.

Dorothy laughed at The Saddle Club's industriousness.

103

"Do you get the feeling we're not necessary?" she asked Nigel.

"It's a nice change," Nigel said. "Perhaps we should hire them."

Stevie looked up, laughing. "Maybe in four years, we'll *all* come live with you."

"Shhh," Carole warned. Kate came back from setting Southwood's saddle against a tree. "Great job, Kate!" Carole said. "You looked fantastic!"

"Southwood was awesome," Lisa added. "We saw you go off that broken bridge. He flew!"

"Thanks," Kate said briefly. She was out of breath and sweating, and she hardly looked at her friends. Most of her attention was on Southwood. Kate checked his legs closely and put her hand on his chest to see how hot he was. "Let's get him walking," she said.

"Wasn't that fun, Kate?" Stevie asked. "I bet you wish you could do that more often." Lisa elbowed her into silence.

"How was it?" Nigel asked.

Kate turned to him. "Fast and clean," she said. "No penalties."

Nigel and Dorothy smiled and. The Saddle Club whooped.

"The favorite, Panache, had a refusal at the water," Nigel told her.

Kate nodded. "I know."

"Most people have had trouble making the time allowed, too," Nigel added.

Kate nodded again. "I know. Southwood was great."

"So were you," Dorothy pointed out. "You're one of the leaders now."

"I know," Kate said simply. The tense expression on her face didn't change. She pulled on Southwood's reins and began to walk him. The Saddle Club followed.

If Dorothy had said that to me, Carole thought, *I would have been thrilled beyond belief. If I had just finished a round like that, on a horse like that, I'd be so happy I wouldn't be able to hold still. I'd hug everyone I saw. At the very least, I'd smile.* She began to feel more concerned about Kate.

"Wasn't that fun, Kate?" Stevie asked again as they walked across the field of grass. This time it didn't sound like a pep talk. This time it sounded like a question. "Was it?"

Kate shook her head. "No," she said. "It wasn't."

They stared at her. "But it should be fun," Lisa said, almost to herself.

Kate turned. "I agree," she said, "but it wasn't. I liked doing it—I guess I'm glad I did it—but it wasn't *fun.*" She paused and bent to wipe a fleck of mud off Southwood's leg. Her friends exchanged glances over her head.

"It should be," Lisa insisted in a whisper. Stevie shrugged.

Carole didn't understand. How could being able to ride

so well be anything but fun? And yet Kate didn't seem to be enjoying herself at all.

AT DINNER NIGEL announced the standings after cross-country. Kate was second in her division, behind Karen and her horse Singalong. Nigel grinned from ear to ear, and the girls leaped from their chairs to hug Kate.

Kate shook her head. "If Karen jumps perfectly tomorrow, then I can't win," was all she said.

"That's right," Nigel replied, looking puzzled. "But you've done your best."

"Not really," Kate said. Her friends didn't ask her to explain. Lisa thought that there were suddenly a lot of things about Kate that she didn't understand. She wasn't even excited about being in second place. Second place! Out of thirty-three! And most of the riders were much more experienced than Kate. Lisa thought that Kate should be thrilled.

Kate knew what she meant when she said she hadn't done her best. She'd tried to fake Karen out before dressage. The glory of her wonderful cross-country ride on Southwood was completely obscured by the memory of the bitter and untrue words she'd said to Karen. Kate sighed. She had promised herself that this event would be different, but it wasn't turning out to be different at all.

106

12

LISA WOKE UP and rolled over sleepily. The illuminated face of the hotel clock shone in front of her: 6:45. Lisa yelped, throwing back the covers. "We're late!" she cried. She snapped on the bedside lamp. "Kate, Kate, we've overslept!"

Kate shot out of bed and frantically began pulling on her breeches. Stevie rushed to help her, yanking Kate's white shirt and stock tie out of the suitcase. In her haste she tripped over the edge of the suitcase and sprawled across the floor. "Stevie!" Carole yelled. She grabbed Kate's shirt and handed it to her, then went back to help Stevie to her feet.

"What time is it, Lisa?" Kate asked. "Why didn't you set

the alarm right? How could you!" She was trying to stuff her uncombed hair into a ponytail. She'd mismatched the buttons on her shirt and the collar bunched beneath her chin.

"Quarter to seven! What happened to the wake-up call?" Lisa wailed.

The others went still. Kate collapsed on the bed with a sigh. Stevie looked down ruefully at the rug burn on her knee, and Carole began to giggle.

"Maybe Dorothy didn't call us because we didn't have to get up until seven," Carole suggested brightly. Stevie began to giggle, too, then Kate, then Lisa. Soon the room roared with laughter.

Kate wiped tears from her eyes. "My heart is still beating so fast," she said. "I think I'm going to die. Lisa, I'm sorry I snapped at you."

"I'm sorry, too," Lisa said. "I saw the clock, and we've been getting up so early . . ."

"It's strange," Stevie said. "Imagine thinking that seven o'clock in the morning is late!"

Kate began to rebutton her shirt. "Since we have a few extra minutes this morning," she said, "I believe I will take the time to brush my hair. And by the way, Stevie, there are Olympic rings carved into the soap in the bathroom. There were Olympic rings dug into the frosting on the cake I had at dinner last night. Olympic rings seem to be following me this weekend." Stevie started to speak, but

Kate held up her hand. "I don't want to know why, not right now. I just wanted you to know that I've noticed."

Carole laughed. She knew Stevie had been drawing Olympic rings wherever Kate might see them, but she hadn't seen the soap. Carole was relieved that Kate looked happier than she had the night before.

THERE WASN'T MUCH to do at the show grounds that morning, even with the early horse inspection. Dorothy checked over Campfire and Southwood closely. Neither horse showed any sign of lameness or injury from the exertions of cross-country.

Kate had had all of the previous afternoon to make sure Southwood was comfortable, to groom him, to rebraid his mane, and to clean his tack. She and the rest of The Saddle Club gave him a quick going-over before the final horse inspection, but they didn't need to do much. Southwood looked magnificent. He trotted out in perfect form, bold and energetic.

"He doesn't look at all tired," Stevie said admiringly as they walked him back to his stall.

"*I'm* tired," Kate said. "Let's take a rest, can we? My show jumping won't be until this afternoon, and I've hardly talked to you guys all weekend. How about a Saddle Club meeting?"

"Sounds great," Carole said. They made Southwood happy in his stall with a full hay net and a handful of carrots, then settled themselves on the grass near the stable.

Kate lay back and stretched herself in the sun. "So nice," she murmured. "Listen, I really haven't been able to spend much time with all of you this weekend, and I wanted to. One of the problems with showing is that it takes so much concentration and work. I hope you aren't upset with me."

"We understand," Lisa said quickly. "This event was really important, not to mention difficult—of course you had to concentrate! We'd never be upset with you about that, Kate."

"We think it's great you got to compete on Southwood," Carole said. "We're glad we were here to watch you do it. You did so well."

"You're in second place going into show jumping," Stevie said. "Think about it, Kate! You could win!"

Kate's face screwed up in sudden agony. Her friends stared at her, shocked. "I am thinking about it," she said. "It's not that I don't want to do well—of course I do—but it seems like all I can think about, at times like this, is winning. Winning, and beating Karen, because right now she's the only person ahead of me. I dreamed last night about it. I woke up this morning and thought about it. I ate breakfast and thought about it. Groomed Southwood and thought about it." She forced a smile. "Sat on the grass and thought about the three of you—my three best friends,"

110

she continued. "You've always been such a good influence on me. If it weren't for you, I would have given up riding entirely. Remember?"

The others nodded somberly.

Lisa pulled the hood of her jacket closer around her face. The wind was still chilly, and the look on Kate's face made her colder still. "Wanting to win isn't bad," she said. "When I'm at a show, I want to win. I'm sure Nigel wants to win."

"I know I do," Stevie added, and the others laughed.

"Yes, but it isn't the *only* thing you think about, Stevie," Kate countered. "It always becomes the most important thing to me. Take this morning. I'm in second place, right? So if Karen has a clean show-jumping round, I can't beat her. At horse inspection, I was thinking it wouldn't be so bad if her horse had maybe just a little cut on its leg from hitting a fence yesterday. Nothing that would hurt it permanently, you understand—just a little cut, something to keep it from passing the inspection today."

Kate's voice broke and her eyes filled with tears. "And that's a horrible thing to think!" she said. "Why would I ever want any horse to fail inspection? And you heard what I said to her yesterday before dressage. She's a very nice person—she loaned me the clothes I'm wearing, and yet I'm lying to her to try to break her confidence. It's no good. I used to do stuff like that all the time, and now, after only one horse trials, it's all coming back. Parts of this event were fun. I love Southwood, and I think he's a great horse. But I'll never do this again."

Kate wiped her face and looked up at her friends with a determined expression. "I gave up competing for good reasons, and I'm not going back."

Lisa, Carole, and Stevie felt stunned. "B-But," Lisa said, stammering a little, "we wanted you to ride in the Olympics!"

Kate stared at her. Her stern expression softened into a smile, and she began to laugh gently. "Me!" she said. "So that's why you kept drawing Olympic rings in things! *You* can ride in the Olympics if you want to. I'll stick to cow ponies. The Saddle Club helped make riding fun for me again, and I'm not about to give that up."

Carole frowned. "Why is it so hard for you, Kate?"

Kate shrugged. "I wish I knew. I don't understand it myself." She paused, then continued, "I've tried to change and I can't, so I guess it's just the way I am. I don't have the right kind of heart to be an Olympic rider. In the end, I'm just not cut out for it."

Carole leaned forward to give her friend a hug. She realized that Kate was making the right choice for herself. "I keep expecting you to think the same way I do," Carole said. "I'm sorry. I can see now why you stopped competing in the first place."

"I'm sorry that our Olympic plans for you won't work out," Lisa added. "But I guess they were *our* plans, not yours, and I know we all understand. I love horses, but I'm not ready to spend my whole life around them, either."

"Me either," Stevie agreed. "I don't like waking up at five every morning. I don't even like six-forty-five." She winked at Lisa.

They laughed. "We still have this competition to finish," Carole said. "I mean, you do, Kate."

Kate shook her head. "'We' is right," she said. "When I saw the way you three looked at me after I was such a snot to Karen, I knew I had to change my attitude. I've been thinking about myself ever since. You really helped."

"Even if we didn't mean to?" Stevie asked.

"Even then."

"It's too bad," Lisa said, "because, you know, we practically had our bags packed for Australia. We were going to go watch you bring home the gold."

"Maybe if Southwood goes, we can all go watch," Kate suggested. "He'll be a great horse, no matter who rides him. Let's go get him ready for show jumping."

United in spirit, they headed for his stall.

STEVIE, HER CAMERA in her hands, stood by the fence that separated the show-jumping arena from the warm-up ring. Her heart thudded with excitement. The afternoon had gone by so quickly! Nigel's horse, Campfire, had ended up in tenth place in his division, and Nigel had been thrilled. Now it was Kate's turn to shine.

The competitors for the advanced division were the last to go, and they jumped in reverse order of standings. That meant that the lowest-placed horse jumped first, and the highest-ranked one—Karen's gray, Singalong—jumped last. Southwood was second to last.

One by one the advanced horses went into the ring. Stevie hadn't paid too much attention to the early ones,

114

since they didn't have a chance of beating Kate. She and Lisa and Carole had done their best to keep Kate laughing and calm. This was Kate's last competition, and they wanted her to enjoy the final day.

Inside the arena, a small black horse tackled the course bravely. Stevie watched him jump a green wall and a wide Swedish oxer, then turn the corner toward the triple combination, a series of three jumps in a row that a lot of horses were knocking down. The black horse jumped the first two parts correctly, then nearly stumbled and hit the third with a crash. Rails fell to the ground. Stevie watched the ground crew rebuild the fence. A sudden thought made her hurry back to the center of the warm-up area.

"Kate," Stevie said, "come watch the next horse go through the triple combination. I think there's something funny about the ground right before the last part. I think that's why so many people are having it down."

Kate trotted Southwood to the edge of the arena. "You're right," she said as she watched the next horse go. "It looks like the ground's gotten torn up by the other competitors. There must be a soft spot there—a puddle or something. But look! The rider can't see the problem until she's already jumped the second fence, and then it's too late to avoid the bad spot."

Kate watched another horse flounder through the triple, scattering rails. "Thanks, Stevie! That's a huge help!"

Now only three riders remained in the warm-up: Kate,

Karen, and the man who was in third. Lisa and Carole set one of the warm-up fences to five feet tall, and Kate popped Southwood back and forth over it a few times. In the show ring the third-place man jumped and had two rails down. It was Kate's turn.

Stevie, Carole, and Lisa clustered by the gate. When Lisa had watched Kate do cross-country, she had thought it was the most exciting thing she'd ever seen; but now her heart beat even faster, because she knew Kate had a chance to win. She realized this event was Kate's last chance, and she really wanted Kate to end her competitive career as a champion.

Kate circled at the far end of the arena, asked Southwood to pick up a canter, and pointed him at the first fence. He jumped beautifully, snapping his knees beneath his chin. They soared over the fences one by one until they came to the triple. Stevie had been taking pictures again, but she lowered her camera. She wanted to see this clearly.

Kate turned wide and approached the first fence far to the left-hand side. She took Southwood through the triple so close to the left sides of the jumps that Carole was afraid Kate's left leg would hit them, but Kate's line avoided the trouble spot in front of the third fence. Southwood jumped the last part of the triple as cleanly and easily as he had jumped the first. Kate and Southwood flew over the final two fences and galloped toward the gate. A perfect round! Kate pulled Southwood up just outside the arena and

116

dismounted into her friends' arms. "You did it!" Carole shouted.

"Here," Kate said in return, thrusting Southwood's reins into Carole's hands. "Hold him for a second—I'll be right back!"

Kate ran toward the gate. She got there just before Karen rode Singalong into the arena. "Karen—stop!" she called. Karen halted her horse and looked at Kate strangely. Kate blushed, knowing that Karen remembered her comments at the dressage ring. But that didn't matter now. "There's a patch of mud in front of the last element of the triple," Kate said breathlessly. "It's slippery and the horses are knocking the fence down. I rode through on the far left side and I got through fine."

Karen grinned. "Thanks," she said. She clucked to Singalong, then pulled him up again. "Thanks a lot," she added. She went into the ring.

Kate went back to where The Saddle Club waited with Southwood. "What did you say to her?" Carole asked.

Kate shrugged. "Nothing much. Let's watch her jump." A strange lightness filled her heart. She hoped that the advice she gave Karen would make up for the rude comments she'd made to her before. She wished it could make up for all the times she'd let her desire to beat people get out of hand. If Karen jumped cleanly, she would beat Kate—but suddenly Kate didn't care. Southwood had jumped clear. He had done his best. Kate had done her best, too. If Karen won, it was simply because she deserved to win.

For the first time in her life, Kate knew that second place would be good enough.

The four girls moved to the gate. Kate took Southwood's reins and stroked his long neck. "You're a champ," she whispered. Karen's horse picked up a canter and jumped the first fences easily. They made the turn to the triple. Karen aimed Singalong wide to the left.

"You told her," Stevie said in amazement.

Kate shrugged and smiled.

"B-But—," Stevie sputtered, "if she goes clean, she wins!"

Singalong jumped the first part clean, and the second, and the third.

"Wow," breathed Lisa. "You didn't have to do that!"

"Yes, I did," Kate said simply. Her friends looked at her. Gradually they realized what she meant. Kate still wanted to win, but this time she didn't want to win at any cost.

"Oh, Kate," Lisa said softly. She felt proud of her friend.

In the ring, Karen turned Singalong toward the second to last fence, and they jumped it easily. She rode toward the final fence—Singalong jumped beautifully—he cleared it—he won.

"Oh, Kate!" Stevie said. She didn't know whether to be happy or disappointed for her friend. Kate had come so close to winning. Kate hugged Stevie, then Carole and Lisa.

"Second place is still amazing," Stevie said, squeezing Kate's arm.

"It is amazing," Kate said, grinning. "I feel great!"

Nigel and Dorothy came running from the stands to congratulate her. Kate accepted their praise happily. *She really feels better this way*, Stevie realized. *She knows Karen won fair and square.*

As if to confirm Stevie's thoughts, Kate said to her, "This feels more like a victory than any class I ever actually won. I did my best, and so did Southwood. He was great!"

In the middle of all the celebration, Karen rode up to Kate, bent down, and held out her hand. Kate shook it heartily.

"Congratulations," Kate said to Karen. "You deserve it."

Karen smiled back. "So do you."

14

THE COLD SPRING rain beat against Lisa's bedroom window in Willow Creek. Lisa sat in her pink armchair, her face covered with chicken pox, studying the photograph of Kate and Southwood jumping the cross-country fence. "It's great," she said, handing it back to Stevie. "They look terrific."

"I'll get copies made for all of us," Stevie promised. "We need to remember the brief return of Kate Devine, Champion Event Rider!"

"But no gold medals," Lisa said. "I really think—well, I really think Kate made the right choice. She knows herself best, after all. Even though she did learn what it takes to be a true champion."

"She also said that she wanted to end on a good note," Carole added. "She wanted to be proud of herself. I can understand that."

"Kate really is a great person," Lisa said. "I know she felt terrible about Beatrice's accident."

"Look at this one," Stevie said, handing another photo to Lisa. Lisa laughed. The photo showed Dorothy and Nigel's stable in North Carolina. The outside door was decorated with yards of blue ribbon—the color of a champion. Another picture showed Southwood's stall, which had been painted blue. A cake sat outside the door.

"Carrot cake," Lisa remembered. "For Southwood and Kate. It was sweet of Drew to decorate like that, after Dorothy phoned him to tell him how Kate did. Drew agreed with the rest of us—he thought Kate's second place was as good as a first. It was a nice homecoming surprise."

"It was a little weird," Stevie said darkly. "The cake and the ribbon were fine, but painting Southwood's stall? That's weird."

"If you'd ever thought of an idea like that, you wouldn't think it was weird," Lisa countered, grinning mischievously. "You'd think it was brilliant."

"If Stevie ever started painting the stalls, Max would have her head," Carole predicted.

"Exactly," Stevie said. "Weird."

"Drew is weird, but he's sweet," Lisa said. "He writes poetry, you know. Nice poems."

121

"What!" Stevie and Carole started laughing. Lisa blushed slightly beneath her pox. "He's written you, like, love poems?" asked Stevie.

"No! Give me a break," Lisa said. "He just sent me a funny verse when Dorothy told him I had chicken pox. I got it yesterday, otherwise I would have told you about it already. He wrote a letter, too, and told me all about Southwood." Lisa sighed. "And he told me, again, how perfect I'd be for his little brother. He wants me to meet him sometime."

"Oh, yuck," Stevie declared. "As if we don't know enough icky boys already. What's his name?"

"Edwin. Drew calls him Eddy."

"Sounds dreadful," said Stevie. "Dorky Drew and Dreadful Eddy."

"Dready Eddy," Carole said.

"Like it matters," Lisa said. "When would I ever meet him anyway? We won't see Dorothy or Nigel anytime soon, let alone Drew, let alone his little brother."

"Here's the last picture," Stevie said, handing it to Lisa.

"Oh!" Lisa said. It was a beautiful shot of Southwood and Kate galloping around the show-jumping ring, taking their victory lap behind Karen and Singalong. A long red ribbon streamed from Southwood's bridle. Kate was smiling. Southwood looked proud, as though he knew how well he'd done.

"When I see that photo, I'm still a little disappointed in

Kate's decision," Carole admitted. "I *know* Kate made the right choice. But Southwood really was fantastic—I think he truly has all the makings of an Olympic horse. And I'm sorry it won't be one of our friends that rides him there."

"But it might be. Think of it, Carole. Dorothy and Nigel bought Southwood," Lisa reminded her.

"That was amazing, really," said Stevie. "Somehow I never thought about Beatrice selling Southwood to Nigel. But she knew Nigel would take good care of him. Beatrice may be human after all."

"So, in four years," said Lisa, "Nigel and Southwood— Olympic bound!"

The phone on Lisa's nightstand rang. Lisa picked it up. "Oh, *Drew*—hi!" she said, turning a little red as her friends burst out laughing. Lisa listened another moment. "Really?" she said. She grabbed the phone with both hands. "Really? *Really?* Wow!"

She covered the receiver with her hand. "Southwood is trying out for the Olympics," she said breathlessly.

"But that's four years—," Carole said.

"Not the next one—this one! This summer!"

"*Really!*" Stevie and Carole shrieked.

"Best of all"—Lisa's face lit up with excitement—"Drew says Dorothy and Nigel have invited us to come along!"

ABOUT THE AUTHOR

BONNIE BRYANT is the author of many books for young readers, including novelizations of movie hits such as *Teenage Mutant Ninja Turtles* and *Honey, I Blew Up the Kid*, written under her married name, B. B. Hiller.

Ms. Bryant began writing The Saddle Club in 1986. Although she had done some riding before that, she intensified her studies then and found herself learning right along with her characters Stevie, Carole, and Lisa. She claims that they are all much better riders than she is.

Ms. Bryant was born and raised in New York City. She still lives there, in Greenwich Village, with her two sons.

GOLD MEDAL RIDERS

Kimberly Brubaker Bradley

EVERY RIDER DREAMS of being part of the biggest horse show in the world: the Olympic Games. Since the modern Olympic equestrian competitions began in 1952, fewer than a hundred Americans have ridden for the gold—and eleven of them have won it. Here are some of their stories.

J. Michael Plumb

Before the opening ceremonies of the 1992 Olympic Games, the American athletes voted to decide which one of them would march first and carry the American flag. The honor went to Mike Plumb, an event rider. He was not as famous as Shannon Miller or Michael Jordan, but he had done something truly amazing. The 1992 Games marked the eighth time that Mike Plumb had been named to an Olympic team—a record no other athlete, in any sport, has ever equaled.

Mike first rode in the 1960 games, and he's been on every Olympic team since, except for 1988, when he was injured just before the Olympic trials. In 1964 he won his first medal, a team silver, in an Olympics marred for him by tragedy.

Mike was to ride a horse named Markham, his mount from the 1960 games. Mike and Markham had been the highest-placed American finishers in 1960, and they were expected to do well again. The 1964 Olympics were in Tokyo. The horses were shipped there by plane, as they are now for every international competition. At the time, however, airplane travel for horses was relatively new.

Markham panicked in midflight and began kicking his stall apart. The people traveling with him were unable to calm him. The pilot, afraid that the horse would kick out the side of the plane and cause it to crash into the ocean, ordered the team veterinarian to put Markham down. He did. Mike landed in Tokyo without a horse.

Left behind in America were two who had tried and failed to make the Olympic team: a man named Bill Haggard, and his horse, Bold Minstrel. Bill was not as good a rider as Mike Plumb, but Bold Minstrel was brilliant. Bill very generously sent Bold Minstrel to Tokyo as Markham's replacement, and Mike rode a solid round on him despite not knowing Bold Minstrel at all. The United States won the team silver medal. (Bold Minstrel later developed a second career as an international show jumper, ridden by Bill Steinkraus.)

Mike's best individual Olympic finish came in 1976, at the games in Montreal. As that Olympics approached, he had a difficult decision to make: Which horse should he ride? He had two to choose from. The first was Good Mixture, a Thoroughbred that had won a silver medal in 1972 with a different rider and had then won gold and silver medals with Mike at the 1974 World Championships. Good Mixture was a great horse that had never had a fault cross-country, but he was getting old.

Better and Better, Mike's other possibility, was the opposite of Good Mixture. He was very young and inexperienced, and although he tried hard, he sometimes had problems on cross-country.

Mike took a chance with Better and Better. He said later that he had "never been prouder of a horse in my life." Better and Better performed as well as he could, and the Americans had never had a higher finish. Mike won the individual silver, finishing just behind his teammate Tad Coffin, and shared the team gold.

Mike Plumb has been riding at the international level for more than thirty-five years, and he still isn't slowing down. Could the 1996 team be his ninth? He hopes so!

William Steinkraus

William Steinkraus was the United States' first show-jumping star. In 1952 he was part of the first modern Olympic team (before that, only army officers could compete). Riding a horse named Hollandia, he helped the United States win a bronze medal. Bill went on to compete in five Olympics on six horses; besides his bronze, he also helped the team win two silver medals in 1960 and in 1972.

His greatest moment came in 1968 at the Olympic Games in Mexico City. Riding a beautiful brown Thoroughbred named Snowbound, Bill became the first American rider ever to win an individual gold medal. Later he said that winning the gold was special because it was not just his victory—he owed a lot to the riders and horses who had gone before him.

After the 1972 Olympics Bill retired from competitive riding. Snowbound, his gold medal horse, was retired at the same time. Bill went on to serve as president of the United States Equestrian Team, and he was the first person inducted into the Show Jumping Hall of Fame. He is still active in the horse world.

Which of his great horses did he like best? "Obviously, Snowbound . . . was a special favorite," he said. "However, I was lucky enough to ride a number of truly outstanding horses—Ksar d'Esprit, Riviera Wonder, Sinjon,

Trail Guide, Bold Minstrel, and Main Spring among them—and I couldn't really pick one of them over the others any more than I could pick a favorite member of my family."

Bill Steinkraus may consider his horses family, but all show jumpers must think of Bill Steinkraus as a father of their sport.

Bruce Davidson

No American has been in more Olympics than Mike Plumb, and only one event rider has been more successful: Bruce Davidson. Like Mike, Bruce has been competing for a long time—he first made the Olympic team in 1972. He has won two gold medals and one silver in his four Olympic attempts, and he's also won the World Championships twice, the Pan American Games, and nearly every other major event in the world. He's often ranked as the best event rider in the world.

Bruce lives on a farm in Pennsylvania with his wife and two children, Buck and Nancy, who are becoming successful riders like their father. His Olympic horses—Plain Sailing, Irish Cap, J. J. Babu, and Dr. Peaches—are all dead now, but all of them, even the ones that never belonged to him, are buried on his farm.

Right now Bruce is riding several new top horses, and one of them might be his next Olympic mount. However, making the Olympics again is not one of his goals. "My goals are to make myself a better rider, to make my horses better, and to make the lives of my horses better," he said. "I do think that I give my horses a better life than they might otherwise have. I let them be successful at something."

Lendon Gray

Not all gold medal riders win gold medals. Lendon Gray has made a terrific impact on the sport of dressage without ever winning an Olympic medal. What Lendon has done instead is take ordinary horses and make them shine. Many people think only big, fancy, expensive horses can do well at dressage. Lendon likes to prove them wrong.

"I think I'm still the only Olympic rider who has only American training and who was riding only American-trained and American-bred horses," she said. Most top American dressage riders go to Europe to train, and they ride imported horses. Lendon rides Arabians. She rides Appaloosas. She rides Morgans. She rides ponies. And with her in the saddle, they all do well.

She made her first Olympic team in 1980, on a horse named Beppo. When she got him, she had never even seen a top-level dressage competition. "I was loaned Beppo when his rider died unexpectedly," she said. "He was not terribly sound, and he was basically a castaway." Lendon learned a lot from Beppo: In four months, the two were competing at the highest levels and won the last spot on the United States' 1978 World Championships team. Two years later they were on the Olympic squad.

Three years after that, Lendon won the U.S. Grand Prix Championship—the highest level of dressage—on her best-known horse, Seldom Seen. Part Thoroughbred and part Connemara, an Irish breed of pony, Seldom Seen was only fifty-nine inches high—one inch taller than a pony! He looked like a midget next to the giant horses he competed against. At first even Lendon didn't expect him to do well.

"Every season I'd think, *This is it*," she recalled. "First he did first and second level. Next we moved up to third and fourth level, and I thought, *Well, any horse ought to be able to do first and second level. This is real dressage now, and we're in over our heads*. He was undefeated at third and fourth levels. Next year we moved up to Prix St. Georges and I thought, *This is it*, but he was undefeated at Prix St. Georges. When we moved up to Grand Prix (international-level competition) I thought, *Well, this is absurd*. He won a record number of national championships."

"I don't do this for the ribbons I can win or for the international competitions," Lendon said firmly, though she competed in the Olympics a second time in 1988. "Right now I'm working with a horse that will probably never be in a show. He's actually what you'd call a physically handicapped horse. The vet said we should put him down, but now he walks and trots and canters comfortably.

"My philosophy in dressage is to take a horse and make it the best that it can be."

Like Mike Plumb, Bill Steinkraus, and Bruce Davidson, Lendon Gray is a gold medal rider.

The author gratefully acknowledges the help of many people, including L. A. Pomery, who handles public relations for the United States Equestrian Team; John Strassburger, publisher of The Chronicle of the Horse; Jo Whitehouse, of the United States Combined Training Association; and Olympic riders Bruce Davidson, Lendon Gray, Lisa Jacquin, Carol Lavell, William Steinkraus, and Jil Walton.

THE SADDLE CLUB

by Bonnie Bryant

Saddle up and ride free with Stevie, Carole and Lisa. These three very different girls come together to share their special love of horses and to create The Saddle Club.

The Saddle Club series is published by Bantam Books.

THE SADDLE CLUB

Why not try reading the SWEET VALLEY TWINS series, also published by Bantam Books.

Meet Elizabeth and Jessica Wakefield – the identical twins of Sweet Valley – and all their friends too. Join in their ups and downs, experiencing the thrills and spills of life in a valley, that is truly amazing!

SWEET VALLEY TWINS™

We hope you enjoyed reading this book. If you would like to receive further information about available titles in the Bantam series, just write to the address below, with your name and address:

KIM PRIOR
Bantam Books
61–63 Uxbridge Road
London W5 5SA

If you live in Australia or New Zealand and would like more information about the series, please write to:

SALLY PORTER
Transworld Publishers (Australia) Pty Ltd
15–25 Helles Avenue
Moorebank
NSW 2170
AUSTRALIA

KIRI MARTIN
Transworld Publishers (NZ) Ltd
3 William Pickering Drive
Albany
Auckland
NEW ZEALAND

All Transworld titles are available by post from:-
Bookservice by Post
PO Box 29
Douglas
Isle of Man
IM99 1BQ

Credit Cards accepted. Please telephone 01624 675137
or fax 01624 670923

Please allow £0.75 per book for post and packing UK.
Overseas customers allow £1.00 per book for post and packing.